THE DRAGON'S FIRE

To Sue —

Thanks for Taking the Chance
with the Book — I hope you enjoy it!

THE DRAGON'S FIRE

David Laird

David Laird

ISBN: 978-1-4834-4321-8 (sc)
ISBN: 978-1-4834-4322-5 (e)

Library of Congress Control Number: 2015920546

Because of the dynamic nature of the Internet, any web addresses or links contained in this book may have changed since publication and may no longer be valid. The views expressed in this work are solely those of the author and do not necessarily reflect the views of the publisher, and the publisher hereby disclaims any responsibility for them.

Any people depicted in stock imagery provided by Thinkstock are models, and such images are being used for illustrative purposes only. Certain stock imagery © Thinkstock.

Lulu Publishing Services rev. date: 1/06/2016

Dedicated to all of those Clydes who descended into the abyss and found the strength and the courage to climb out

Beware the fire of the dragon that it won't consume you.

1

Clyde hadn't slept in weeks—hell, seemed like months. Meds no longer working, booze refusing to cooperate, best friend gone, wife packing up. When he was dead, he figured, she would quickly hook up with Pete, maybe even Merlin. Didn't matter. Whatever she did, she would be better off without him.

He finished preparing the blankets and placed the .22 rifle on top. Bear was next to him, his constant companion. Clyde sat and began petting him. A tear ran down his face as he lay down to gently stroke the dog's nose, slowly moving his hand past Bear's face and settling it behind his ear. Bear rolled over for a stomach scratch, so Clyde obliged.

The room was small, dark, hidden under the basement stairs. It was the size of a closet, but tonight its use would be far different. He wanted this moment to be timeless; he didn't want to move forward, yet he was unable to look back. So he lay there, stroking his dog and thinking how safe he felt in his open tomb. "Why did they all leave us?" he mumbled.

A tear nourished his resolve; he rose from his cocoon and stumbled upstairs. His depression had deepened to a point of no return, with no one left who seemed to care. His anger intensified as he remembered Pete Everhart. What a friend! Turned him on to Merlin Sanders, his Percocet doctor—Mr. Magic Fucking Man, who had guided them on their mind numbing journey until Everhart decided to desert him, just like all his other so-called friends, to get the cure. What the hell kind of friend was that?

Should have pulled the trigger on Valentine's Day, he thought. *That would have showed 'em. Love ya', honey. Blam.* Valentine red splashed over all her favorite shit, the back of his head sprayed over everything his duplicitous wife ever valued. Perfect, if he'd had any balls. *Yeah, that would have showed 'em.*

Lighting a cigarette, he coughed and stared out the kitchen window at the darkening, steely sky. *Perfect day to check out and finally be done with everything.* He took another long, patient drag and exhaled as he thought of Dags, his traitorous friend. *He fucking tells my family I do drugs? What the fuck does he do, that fucking bastard?* The coughing fit returned as he stubbed out his cigarette.

His tears strengthened as he screamed, "Why would he do that to me?

Bear simply stared and panted.

Snatching at his receding anger, Clyde spewed, "Fuck! I've got secrets on him I could have blared to the world. But no, I kept quiet because he was my friend. Nobody understands friendship anymore. Fuck 'em, fuck 'em all! I'm not missing tonight."

He began to move around the house with a kind of serenity he really hadn't felt in a lifetime. He knew what he had to do, what he wanted to do. The sudden calm was a euphoric high he had never encountered.

He hadn't been ready the last time. Valentine's Day—a fruitless cry for help or a dry run? Maybe a little of both. You know, check out the taste of the barrel—thick, cold, flinty. Position it properly, feeling the gun sight caress the roof of his mouth, causing a feather-like tickle, and gauging the sensitivity of the trigger. He had felt a surge of adrenalin that was stronger than any drug-induced rush he had ever experienced, but he had been unprepared for it and so drew back. Not tonight. Tonight he would welcome that surge. He must. He would embrace the moment. In a twisted way, he needed to stay focused. Joanne was working late, or so she said, giving him plenty of time to perfect his exit.

Why was she leaving him? She had promised to stay and give him love and support. She used to love his lifestyle. They had been great together. They both loved to drink, and they both loved his meds. What changed her to make her walk out when he needed her most? Was it Pete? Was it someone else? Or was she simply tired of him? He no longer cared. He looked down into Bear's questioning eyes, kneeling down to meet them. He accepted a lick on the chin and asked, "Why is our Honey Bear leaving us? Why is she leaving me?"

Pete had been his oldest friend. They had shared booze, drugs, and women their entire lives, culminating with his introduction to Pete's pain management doctor, Merlin Sanders. Sanders would wave his magic wand, and Clyde's pain—physical and emotional—would vanish. Soon Clyde was exchanging top-shelf weed for one hundred Percocet, so he, Joanne, and Pete could groove to the painkilling hum of the perfect drug.

He lit another cigarette, replacing the cough with an involuntary gulp. Bear wanted more attention, so he began rubbing the dog's nose, all the while infusing the outside deepening dusk into his soul. "Why did Pete quit?" he mumbled.

Why had Pete left him to deal with these demons alone? They were supposed to have been simpatico in all this. Now he was on his own, taking more and more pills, sometimes ten a day, sometimes twenty, feeling so strung out that even a handful of sleeping pills weren't helping. Clyde couldn't believe he wasn't dead already. Soon, very soon.

He rose, angry that Sanders had cut him off after realizing he'd unleashed a drug-craving monster. Christ, the whole world had turned against him.

As Clyde moved around the house, his eyes settled on a photo of himself and Dags, taken after a round of golf. He picked up the frame and unconsciously caressed it with his thumb. There he was, smiling with his best friend, now his greatest betrayer. Years ago, he had subconsciously put Dags on a pedestal. He'd idolized the entire Bissell family, for that matter, but in the end, they had all just dumped him. Dags had hung him out to dry when he called Clyde's despicable brother about his drug use. Great guy!

Then Pete had come over on Valentine's Day and talked him out of killing himself, removing the shotgun and telling him to dry out. Just like that—dry out. Didn't they know he couldn't fucking dry out? His two greatest friends had independently ganged up on him.

Everybody had seen his .22 rifle, which he'd mounted on the wall like a trophy kill. But instead of being the victim, it would become the hunter tonight. Maybe they thought the gun was harmless; maybe they just didn't care. He knew that must be it, and when he checked out, everyone else would be better off.

He went into the bathroom and looked in the mirror. His hollow, dark face and sunken, tortured eyes accented his naturally gaunt frame. How had that visage come to such a place? He saw one of her lipsticks, removed the cap, and smelled the scent that used to drive him wild. *God, we used to be good together!* He closed his eyes and inhaled. Then, opening his eyes as he exhaled, he extended the tube and began writing on his reflection, scrawling large letters across his predeceased face in a steady, rehearsed hand: "How could you leave?"

He found a bottle of Xanax and swallowed what was left, not even bothering with water or vodka. Then he went downstairs to mix one final drink—lots of vodka with a splash of soda in a tall glass. He peered outside. The early spring dusk resembled gray steel, reminding him of the inviting taste of the muzzle yet to come.

Then he picked up the phone and called the man solely responsible for this moment. Dags's wife answered. Clyde really didn't want to make small talk—this was strictly business—so he simply asked for Dags. A moment later, he heard the distinctive voice of his betrayer, a simple "Hello."

Clyde knew what to say; he had even practiced it. "Dagger, thanks for ruining my life." He hung up, not the least bit interested in further conversation.

He could almost taste the coming moments, feeling sheer excitement mixed with some trepidation, coated with the alluring promise of peace. *Be strong this time. Be strong,* he urged himself as he opened the cellar door and descended the steep steps, ducking to miss the ceiling that he had hit so many times before when he was happily loaded.

Bear followed him down, not knowing what adventure lay in store. Bear, his last friend, another dumb, loyal retriever who would follow his master to hell and back, if allowed. Tonight Bear was not going to follow him to hell. Clyde would go alone.

A single lamp lit the way to his cave, throwing shadows across his workbench and, beyond that, a cracked, green leather couch that faced an old, unused TV. He slowly took in his surroundings one final time, his eyes settling on a photo of Joanne and him on their wedding day. Two strangers smiled back. He lingered another moment, locked on a forgotten time in his past, before turning to enter his haven.

The gun lay on the blankets, locked and loaded, silently inviting him to sit. He acquiesced. He raised his glass to Bear, emptied it, and picked up the gun—the gun he had owned as a child, the gun that would, he hoped, cleanly end his life now. He gave Bear a final hug and a kiss, took a long, slow breath, and placed the muzzle in his mouth. Taking his final breath, he closed his eyes, and left this world as violently as he had entered it.

After Clyde's phone call, and not knowing his intentions, I talked it over with my wife, Katy, and we figured I'd better drive over and confront him. Yeah, I'm Dags—Dags Bissell. Some call me Dagger. My dad named me after the Norse god Dagr, even though he was of Swedish descent. Part Scottish, part Swedish, an obvious product of marauding northern Europeans. And now part pissed and part curious.

I hopped in the car and stretched the thirty-minute drive into forty-five as I reminisced about our fractured friendship and tried to formulate a plan to handle our anticipated confrontation. Clyde might not even open the door for me. I was tired of being pissed off at him and tired of him being pissed off at me. Maybe we could begin mending our relationship tonight. For once I was going to be patient, or at least try to be. Having yet to be canonized as a saint, I have always had an uneasy relationship with patience.

Clyde had come to visit us at our winter home in Ponte Vedra, Florida, ten months earlier, and his deteriorating condition was obvious. He had the red puffy face of a northerner who went to Jamaica and forgot to use sunblock—sort of like an overripe beefsteak tomato—except Clyde hadn't even left Philadelphia. His heart was in overdrive pumping blood to his face, head, and drug-addled brain. If he had said "Hi" and then fallen over dead, I would have been shocked but not surprised.

I quickly realized why. He was chewing Percocet and drinking vodka at a rate that I would have found impressive if I had been a scientist studying the effects of drug interactions on humans. But I wasn't a scientist, and Clyde was my old friend who was spiraling downward toward nothing good. When the weekend ended and he was packing to leave, he thanked me for a great time. My only response was to say I wished he didn't do so many drugs. He shrugged and walked away.

Suffering from that common human affliction called "I think I know everything," I decided to initiate an intervention with Clyde's family. Not his wife—I knew she wouldn't buy into it—but his father and brother, with whom he worked in a successful family business. My phone call the next morning set in motion the series of events that would bring me here tonight.

Two knocks on the door elicited no response except Bear barking. I tried the knob; the door was unlocked. I opened it, calling Clyde's name, and knew right away that something was wrong. A faint aroma of cordite wafted to my nostrils, raising the hair on my neck. *Oh shit. Oh no.* Bear led me to the stairs down to the basement. I followed, already knowing what I'd find at the bottom of the stairs. I no longer needed Bear to guide me. I simply followed the scent to a recess behind the stairs.

There he lay. The motherfucker had shot himself. I collapsed next to him and held his hand, covering his shattered head with a corner of the blanket. His hand was still warm. Bear came over and sat on his other side, resting his head on Clyde's knee. I looked at the dog.

"You were here, weren't you, boy?" I whispered. "You witnessed it, didn't you?" I met Bear's curious, tilted stare. "How could he do this? Did the sound scare you?" I took my other hand and began petting him before continuing. "How did I not see this coming?"

Had I been such a terrible friend that I didn't even know Clyde was capable of this? How had he gotten to a place so bad that he felt the only escape was chewing on a bullet?

I returned my gaze to his covered face. "With all your friends willing to help, you had to do this? What a fucking asshole you are!" My anger was intensifying. I yanked the blanket off and screamed, "What the fuck were you thinking?" I was staring at someone I had hated for nearly a year and now desperately missed.

I couldn't figure out the look on his face. Naively, I had expected to see a man at peace, released from a life that had apparently become hell on earth. What I saw instead was a little confusing, other than the expected carnage. His look could have been one of "I really did it" or maybe "What the fuck did I just do?" It really didn't matter to me. I guess I was using pathology to mask my confused feelings at having lost an old friend.

Bear had pressed himself to my side until he was nearly sitting on top of me, insisting that I pet him. I know dogs are resilient, but I suspect he was scared and searching for comfort from the nearest human. I stroked his head gently, buried my face in his golden fur, and cried.

Clyde's phone call haunted me. He hated me for what I had done to him. He viewed it as the ultimate disloyalty, and as a result, I was "dead to him." Yeah, he watched too much TV, loved *The Sopranos* and the tough talk, but he really was nothing more than a sensitive guy with a raging drug problem. And if I was dead to him, why did he call? My wife had answered the phone and handed it to me, saying, "I think it's Clyde." I said hello and heard his voice for the first time in nine months and the last time ever. "Dagger, thanks for ruining my life," he said, and then he hung up without giving me a chance to reply. Just like that, it was over.

I know—why didn't I call him back? Who knows? My immediate reaction was confusion and then, after a few moments to digest what I had heard, anger. Not knowing or even suspecting his motive, I was just angry that he would call me and unleash such negativity over something I had done so long ago and then hang up without allowing me a response. Granted, my response might have been a simple "Fuck you!" and a similar hang up on him. Two can play these childish games, and our fractured relationship would have given me an ample excuse to lower myself to his level. But that never happened. He said what he wanted to say, and I was left with the phone in my hand, speechless.

Clyde was never able to grasp the idea that I was trying to help him when I called his brother to discuss his diminishing health, so any response I might have made to his phone call would have gone unanswered. As I soon discovered, he had an agenda that night—a script, if you will—to follow:

- Scrawl a note on the mirror to my wife.
- Call Dagger.
- Say good-bye to my dog.
- Get comfortable and blow my fucking brains out.

Mission accomplished. No, nothing I could have said or done that night was going to alter the outcome. At least that was the line I fed myself.

Looking back at it now, I believe—no, I know—that in a bizarre and macabre way, he was reaching out to me, his old, deceitful friend, almost in an "Et tu, Brute?" manner. I was the last person he talked to, and that is a "forever" bond we will always have. Of course, it crossed my mind more than once that his aim was to create a lifetime of guilt or remorse for me, but he failed at that as surely as he'd failed at life. Again, that was the line I fed myself.

How could one of the most fearless guys I'd ever known when we were younger end up like this? Now that I think about it, putting a loaded gun in your mouth with the intention of firing it could be construed as a fearless act. Desperate, but fearless.

My first reaction was anger, on so many levels: anger at the violent act, anger that he would call and leave such a virulent message for my brain to process for the rest of my life, and especially anger that he'd reached this decision without any of his close friends knowing how much he was suffering.

After gathering some of my shattered senses together and before calling 911, I slowly made my way upstairs, ducking to miss an outcrop of cement that held a small overhead closet. Clyde had been so proud of his house, which was a testament to professional success that I found surprising considering what I was looking at now. I was obviously in shock. As I walked, Bear never far from me, I lovingly examined Clyde's personal knickknacks as I came across them— mostly photos of his many friends in various stages of happiness or, more to the point, inebriation. One photo especially caught my eye. I remembered the moment well. We had finished a brutal game of golf, brutal because of the amount of cocaine and alcohol we had consumed. We sported exuberant smiles and held crossed drivers. We were buddies then, best friends. You could see it in our faces. And despite our current estrangement, he still displayed many photos of us during happier times. He used to make people laugh uproariously. What happened to him?

As I approached the bathroom, the note to Joanne screamed at me from the mirror. She was going to leave him, or maybe she'd already gone. Why? Then I saw the open vanity drawer littered with prescription bottles, most of them empty. Sleeping pills: Ambien, Halcion, and Restoril; antianxiety drugs: Valium, Librium, and Xanax; and the painkillers: Oxycodone, Percocet, and Vicodin. Quite an array for one guy. Thirty, maybe forty bottles—too many to count—and many prescribed by one doctor, Merlin Sanders.

I pulled out my cell phone and numbly dialed 911 as I pocketed a representative sample of his latest and final addictions. When the operator answered, I was at a loss for words. How do you tell a total stranger that you are looking at your friend who just shot himself in the head? Still in a fog, I mumbled something about a shooting, a suicide, and a dead body. Then I hung up and returned to the bathroom mirror.

"How could you leave?" The questioning plea stared at me the way Clyde had stared at it a short time ago. One phone call, one message, two men connected, staring in the same mirror moments apart. One dead, the other ... I recognized the handwriting. Showing neither anger nor desperation, it simply mirrored the man who now lay dead in the basement. My eyes penetrated his message and came to rest on my own image. A man in shock returned my gaze through the lipstick, just as the man before him had done as he wrote the note to his wife while planning his phone call to me.

A pack of cigarettes lay on the vanity next to the still-extended lipstick. I reached for it. I hadn't smoked in years, yet those cigarettes, Clyde's cigarettes, beckoned. I pulled one out and lit up, unleashing a long-forgotten coughing fit. Smoke covered the mirror, masking the image and breaking the spell. I took another drag, this one a little better as it brought me closer to my friend, went back to the living room, and tried to get comfortable. As I reached for an ashtray, the front door opened and Joanne walked in.

"What the hell are you doing here?" she nearly hissed. "Get out of our house, now!"

"I came over because Clyde left me a cryptic message an hour ago and I needed some clarification," I replied, really wanting to say, "Congratulations, you bitch. You finally killed him."

"Where is he?" she asked, looking around.

"He's down in the basement. Joanne … he's dead."

She dropped her purse and raced to the basement door, Bear at her heels. I stayed put—in hindsight, maybe not such a good idea, since she hated me, her husband was dead, and there was a loaded gun in the basement. Her scream was punctuated by the sirens of the police cars and ambulance racing up the drive.

3

By the time I got home, having given a statement to the police and listened to Joanne venting that it was all my fault—I guess she had a hard time reading or understanding mirror English—I was pretty wiped out and just wanted to drink a few beers while I tried to come to terms with the most horrifying and bizarre night of my life. I began to understand that being the first to find Clyde was as darkly unique to me as placing his last phone call to me had been to him. I'm quite certain that some shrinks I've had in the past would have a field day with such a symbiotic relationship.

Katy walked into the room in her nightgown. *Shit! I forgot to call Katy.*

"How is he?" she asked, coming over to sit next to me. "You look like you've just seen a ghost. What happened?"

"I have," I stammered. "Honey, the ghost was Clyde, and he's dead. He shot himself, Katy. He called me, and then he shot himself. The fucker shot himself! I saw his body, Katy, I saw his head, I saw his mouth … there was so much blood."

Katy gasped, and I began to shake as she hugged me. My avalanche of emotions came crashing out in a cacophony of cries, shrieks, and moans. Nine months of pent-up feelings spewed forth in a raw display I hadn't shown since my father died eight years earlier. He was the first dead person I ever saw, but as he died the day before I saw him, I was prepared for the emotional turmoil that I experienced. Clyde was obviously different. I was completely unaware of his situation, he was an estranged friend, and he'd put a bullet in his brain. Yeah, pretty different.

As I began to calm down, Katy pulled away and said, "You know, he was an incredible asshole to say that to you and then commit suicide. He wanted to pull you down with him for eternity. What a coward!"

She rose from the couch and went to make herself a drink and get me a beer. When she returned, I could see how angry she was. She'd had time to assimilate the night's incident and conclude that Clyde wanted to kill me by ruining my life the way he thought I had ruined his. She knew those final words from him might lead me to the brink of a breakdown.

"How could he say that to you? What kind of man, what kind of a friend attacks someone like that? What a fucking asshole!"

"Honey, I've got to believe he was reaching out to me—not in spite, but to say good-bye. I have got to believe that. It's the only way I can get past this and survive."

"Well, he was a sick man who lashed out at my husband, and for that I will never forgive him. May he roast in hell!"

That Katy! If you fuck with her, or especially me, she will hold a grudge against you for all of this life and much of the next. People like Katy take "faithful wife" to a whole different level.

I finally calmed her down and convinced her to go to bed, but I stayed up to have a few more beers and try to figure out how the hell I'd gotten to this place—reminiscing about Clyde, his family, and the connections I had with them both.

My thoughts flew to Clyde's father, a cool, dapper guy I had loved being around. He managed to be profane yet sophisticated—a true art form that I've tried to perfect for years, unsuccessfully of course, as my immense use of profanity overwhelms what little sophistication I think I might possess. He reminded me of Sean Connery—balding, six feet one, and 190 pounds, with a glint in his eye that hinted at things he knew that we could only dream about. Very confident, very handsome, and very cold. I never understood the "very cold" part until I talked with him about his son. Only then did I realize my mistake, but by then it was too late.

It all goes back to my call. That call. Why did I make a call that effectively ended a human being's life? How could I have been so arrogant as to think that a call to his brother, who passed it along to a father with no love for his son, would be beneficial to the son, my old, sick friend, Clyde? I was a fool, but I didn't know the complexities of Clyde's relationship with his father. Or if I did, I unconsciously chose to ignore them.

I kept reminding myself that I made the call out of love, to ask the brother to alert their father about his sick and needy son. And yet there was anger in my call, as well—anger from years of putting up with Clyde's addictive shit, his bringing drugs to our parties and offering painkillers to anybody and everybody, his falling down, his public embarrassments. Yes, I had put up with enough. I was angry and ready to offer my own version of tough love.

That anger began to percolate again as I thought of my mistakes, so I rose and walked out to the porch, grabbing another beer along the way. I listened to the nighttime sound of a great horned owl searching for any friends or mates who still might be up, the mournful hoo, hoo-hoo, hoo, hoo of an animal craving the company of his fellow sleepless. I returned its call and returned to my musings.

Mistakenly believing that Clyde's father cared, I initiated a series of phone calls over the next few days. During those conversations, I learned more about Clyde's relationship with his father than I had known from the previous thirty years of our friendship. Clyde's father was also his boss, and the more we spoke, the more I came to realize that he was more of a boss than a father. He never exhibited to me any compassion or concern for his son's addictions or health problems. Maybe he cared at one time and grown tired of worrying about them; maybe he never cared. He kept repeating that he had to wear two hats and was responsible for thirty employees. He also related Clyde's many mistakes in the company, the most egregious being a year earlier, when he had overdosed on Percocet and missed work for several weeks. Clyde had kept this episode from us, refusing to discuss it with anyone. Knowing what I now know, I believe that this was the beginning of Clyde's depression stemming from his addictions. His wife knew it, his friend Pete Everhart knew it, and his father and brother knew it, but their cabal of silence kept this information from Clyde's true support group—me and my brother Jack and his family—as well as other concerned friends.

When his father told me he'd decided to cut Clyde loose from the company if he didn't get treatment, his words sent chills to the very core of my being. They also pissed me off and scared the hell out of me. If that came to pass, Clyde would lose his only motivation to stay sober. And I knew such an ultimatum wouldn't sit well with him; Clyde didn't like to be bullied. I now believe his father knew exactly what he was doing, with the anticipated result of getting Clyde out of the company. Clyde and his father never spoke again.

What kind of a father does that to his son? What kind of son reacts that way to his father?

Clyde's father suffered a stroke two months after their estrangement and died after an additional four months in the ICU ward of a stroke rehabilitation center. I later learned that during that time, neither father nor son showed any remorse or interest in renewing contact. Clyde never visited his father in the hospital, and he didn't attend his father's funeral. His brother's payback for this snub was to omit Clyde from his father's obituary, a long one that went into great detail about his academic, business, social, and family history. The longer it went on, the more overt the omission became. Was the father-son schism a case of a lifetime of psychological abuse by a parent, one of a son never accepting the responsibilities of adulthood, or both?

Clyde never looked within to assign responsibility for his problems. I was dead to him the moment I made the call. His father was dead to him the moment Clyde made his choice. His wife and Pete were dead to him the moment they chose a different life's path that did not include him. With his world crumbling around him because of his own bad decisions, he blamed everybody but himself and committed suicide.

My mind began to wander from Clyde's father to my own. Our fathers, though of the same social status, couldn't have been more different. As the oldest of six, I was a test case for my parents, and the three of us spent many years trying to figure each other out. Verbalizing my feelings about my father has been a challenge for me since the day he died. Over the past eight years, I've mentally catalogued snippets of my feelings in order to paint an honest portrait of a man I dearly loved.

My father was a humble man with a brilliant mind that was active and flexible to the end. He possessed a thirst for knowledge nonpareil for a man of his or any generation. His selflessness, which led him to work with many charities, began at home with his loyalty to his family. Whatever he did, he did for us. The longer he lived, the more he came to appreciate my mother and their six children.

His was a life well lived. In his younger years, he was a world traveler who climbed the Matterhorn, witnessed bullfights in Spain, and crewed sailboats in ocean races. When he wasn't at his desk working, he was instilling in us his thirst for adventure. He was a connoisseur of fine wine, and like a great wine, he aged well.

Fatherhood was a learning experience for him; there were some setbacks along the way, beginning with yours truly. I was new to the world, and he was new to the often-frustrating task of raising a family—a task that gave him a head of gray hair at a very early age. We spent our lives turning a contentious relationship into one of mutual love and admiration. He grew as a father with every child, and the older he got, the more precious our relationship became. It was almost as if he knew his time might be short, so he relished every moment with each of us.

I visited my father four months before he died. I sensed he wasn't doing well and felt that I needed a generous dose of love from him in case I never saw him again.

During a phone call two weeks before he died, I lost my temper with him over a perceived omission on his part. As I have been prone to do my entire life, I jumped to the wrong conclusion. Moments later I realized my mistake. I called him back, apologized for what

I had said, and told him what a special father, mentor, and friend he had been to me. I think I embarrassed him, but he told me how much he loved me and how proud he was to have me as a son. I again said, "I love you, Dad," and hung up feeling so fulfilled in our relationship. That was the last time we spoke.

When my mother called at dawn on March 15, the Ides of March, with the news of his death, I reverted to my childhood. After stumbling around the living room, numb and silently screaming, I woke Katy and told her my daddy died. Then I burst into tears.

The next day when I saw him at the funeral home, he was lying on a gurney dressed in his baby-blue striped pajamas. He looked asleep; he didn't have the mannequin-like appearance that dead people have if they are going to be preserved for a few days. For that I was thankful. I noticed that his last breath had been a struggle, as his lips were drawn tight. Only later did I learn that the mortician had sewn them closed, as people's mouths tend to relax and fall open in death. I touched his cold hands and caressed his pale face, telling him what a wonderful father he had been. Then I said good-bye, hoping that one day we would meet again.

We met again that night in a dream. Both my parents were there, looking young and happy, and they were standing on the other side of an unidentified chasm. My dad was motioning for me to come over and join them. I just watched them, not moving, not replying, as though I were watching a movie. I woke up crying as the reality of his death freshened in my semiconscious state. My crying intensified as I realized that he had blessed me with a visit, as he always would in my times of need.

Thus began a quiet, internal quest, not for the meaning of life but for the importance of death at the moment of death. When it approaches, how do we react? Do we lose all fear of death when it is inevitable, or do we fight for that final, instinctive breath? Is death easier for the religious because they believe in the hereafter, while atheists face a dark void? Or is it the polar opposite, the religious having second thoughts while the atheists relish the end they have always seen coming? For the chronically ill, death should be a blessing, shouldn't it? Maybe not. One of the many directives of hospice is to help the patient accept death by resolving lingering issues in life. Initial anger about the diagnosis evolves into sadness and ultimately acceptance of the illness as a preparation for death. So says the booklet, but that's not always true. Many people never resolve their anger, and they basically die kicking and screaming, with family members pumping morphine into them as a not-so-subtle form of euthanasia.

Do homicide or accident victims have the time or energy to face death as it comes, or do they simply take a final breath and die? Does the homeless man accept death as nobly as, or maybe more nobly than, the materially wealthy man, knowing that at the moment of death, all men are once again equal? To state the absurdly obvious, we only die once, so how do we face death, how do we accept it? And since we only do it once, is it worthwhile to do it well—to look death in the eye, so to speak?

Suicide allows the victim not only to accept death on his terms, but to invite it. He can pick the time, the place, and the method. He has total control of the way he leaves this world, and yet he has lost total control of his life. In a sense he has already died and is simply awaiting the formality of death.

So is the suicide victim really a victim? Can people who have complete control over their deaths be called victims when they murder themselves? I don't pretend to know anything about the psychology of suicide; I simply wonder why so many friends of mine have chosen to stick guns in their mouths and pull the triggers.

Were they so desperate in life that they were willing to put guns in their mouths and fire, not caring about the carnage they would leave to their loved ones? Or were they so crazy from their problems that they put guns in their mouths and fired, not knowing about the carnage they would leave to their loved ones?

Quite often, suicide is ritualized. *Seppuku* is the traditional Japanese suicide ritual; a disgraced man would disembowel himself before a trusted friend decapitated him. I tend to steer clear of swordsmen as friends for that very reason. As poignant as the act portrayed in *Shogun* might be, I'm partial to the "Suicide Is Painless" scene in *M*A*S*H*. Painless is a well-endowed dentist who has failed sexually with a nurse. He feels that his life is over, spinning out of control, and so he asks Hawkeye how to commit suicide. Hawkeye gives him a black pill, which is really just a sleeping pill. Painless takes it and lies in a coffin to die, presumably painlessly. In the meantime, Hawkeye has enlisted a short-timer nurse to cure Painless's sexual inadequacies. She does so and is seen leaving Korea with a look of satisfied wonderment on her face. If every suicide "victim" were able to opt for the black pill, I believe many would wake up the next day and reconsider.

But life is not *M*A*S*H*. When a person's life begins to disintegrate, a black pill probably won't work. Where was Clyde's mind the night he died? Did he feel he had no choice, or was it a "Fuck you, world!" choice that he made? Was he a victim, or was he a murderer?

I've come to believe that on the night Clyde died, his life was unsalvageable short of someone physically dragging him away and having him committed for several months. Even then, who knows? He may have checked out clean, gone home, and blown his brains out as a way of tying up some unfinished business. After all, he had no support system in place, no job, no family, no future, and the taste of steel still lingering on his breath. Could I really blame him?

4

Sterling felt her mind go into vapor lock. Her latest romance novel had come to a crashing halt once she heard the news about Clyde Colson. Her old friend and former lover was dead—suicide. The words to her lighthearted romp had simply dried up as a nearly forgotten past reemerged. They had flowed from her brain to her laptop as easily as a mountain stream meanders through highlands and forests to the valley below … until now. She reread the last couple of pages, hoping to regain some continuity or attitude or whatever it was that allowed her to create.

She felt a smile cross her face as she looked to the window toward the water. He had gone to the dock to find whatever catch had come in that day— grouper, mahi, swordfish, something plain as day or more exotic. It didn't matter. They always enjoyed each other, regardless of the catch.

She was dying for a glass of chardonnay but was determined to wait for him to return, open the bottle, and pour her a glass, as she loved to watch him do. What was it about watching him? Was it their limited time together, their forbidden love making every moment special? He was so sexy—that steady voice that grounded her, that reliable style, that openness combined with certainty. He was her rock, but she was a pretty good rock herself. She kept him laughing, as he did her. She never tired of his thoughtful, attentive conversation, and though her antics ranged from loving to teasing to daring, it amused him to have so much life and joy around him.

Sterling was feeling like a chardonnay but didn't have the luxury of waiting for someone to come home, so she rose from her desk and went to the kitchen to open a bottle of Ferrari-Carano. She poured a glass, threw in a couple of cubes, and returned to the story. She was feeling better reading it, even though she already knew the ending.

While she waited, she came up with the plan, stifling a giggle as it crystallized in her head. She was an adventurous eater, willing to try everything, so she needed to figure out a special dish—something romantic! She barely had time to jump in the car and drive to the local market. She was counting on him to run into a couple of buddies and have a beer. *What to buy ... hmmm, maybe some oysters for an appetizer?* The idea made her laugh, so she bagged a couple dozen. Maybe add some mango salsa for some sashimi or fish tacos? She grabbed a mango, a papaya, an avocado, and some limes. This was going to be fun!

She hastened back to the cottage and dashed to the bedroom, searching for that silk scarf he always liked to feel against her skin. She really wanted that glass of wine! It seemed like he was gone a long time, but it gave her the opportunity to get everything ready. The mango was perfectly ripe, as was the avocado. She cut open the papaya and took a bite. It was to die for!

She started to feel that old twinge of concern. What if something had happened? What if he didn't come back? She loved him so and wanted their limited time together to go on forever. They had already missed so much. She knew she was "horrible-izing," thinking the worst when the worst never happened. But it strengthened her love for him all the same.

She headed for the wine, about to break her promise to herself, just as that big grin came in the door. She felt herself catch her breath, just like the first time they met and every day since.

He laughed as he tossed her a package of ahi tuna, sashimi grade, a package of hog snapper, and a package of Mahi. "Strut your stuff, babe, while I get cleaned up." Turning to leave, he paused, then returned to give her a kiss, a soft kiss, lips barely touching, and then another, a little deeper. God was he sensual! She knew where this was leading, but not yet. She pushed away.

"After we eat," she whispered, wondering why she was waiting.

"But I want to eat now," he said, flashing her that crooked smile.

She returned his smile. "Later you can have as much as you want," she replied, forcing herself to turn away.

"Then let me pour you a glass of wine," he said. "I don't want you to be thirsty while you create, but fish is not really what I'm hungry for."

Just as she had hoped he would, he opened a bottle of wine and poured her a glass, throwing in a couple of cubes and bringing it to her as if she were the most precious woman in the world. She was far from perfect, but it felt good to be loved.

Sterling had forgotten how good it felt to be truly loved. Clyde's friend Dags Bissell had been one of those loves from a long ago, forgotten time, and she had based many a hero on his idealized qualities— tall, strong, chiseled face, dark hair, and piercing emerald eyes, the look of many until he looked at her. She thought about her daughter's father and wondered what he looked like now. She imagined a head of salt-and-pepper hair and more facial scars to accompany the ones she remembered, a testament to his rowdy youth. He had never backed down from a confrontation, and more often than not, the ensuing skirmish resulted in new friendships and rounds of drinks.

When her relationship with Clyde had run its course, her friendship with his best friend had remained and slowly blossomed. One night after too many friendly drinks, they had gone home together, and her life was never the same. She'd thought their love would last forever, but it didn't. One day he was gone with barely a "See ya" to end it. Her broken heart and soon-discovered pregnancy led her to explore an untapped creativity that evolved into a decent living as a romance novelist in Boca Grande, Florida. She was one of the few residents who weathered the summer, but that was her creative time. The solitude, even the oppressive heat of the gulf, helped her write. She was such a romantic; it was easy for her to fall for the men she created and thus live a relatively solitary life writing and raising her daughter. With Clyde's death, the unknowing father of her child was back in the picture. She poured another glass and returned to her manuscript with a smile.

> Their fingers touched as he handed her the glass, and he laughed, grabbed her around her waist, and pulled her close to give her a kiss. She gently pushed him away with a look that promised him heaven, later, after his shower. He shot her that grin and walked into the bedroom. God, should she follow? It would be so easy, and they could always encore after dinner. No. It was time to prepare.
>
> The food would take no time at all, but the atmosphere had to be special—no, perfect. She

carefully placed colored floor pillows along two sides of the room so they could rest against the walls while they ate. The big quilt that they used for picnics served as a table, and thick, lavender-scented candles pulled it all together.

Whew, that's done, she thought as she made her way back to the kitchen. She sliced the fish for sashimi, wondering how the mahi would taste. She tried a piece with avocado, lime, and a thin slice of red onion. Wow!

He walked out of the bedroom, wrapped in a towel, drying his hair.

God, you're an idiot, she thought, but got hold of herself. "Honey, I'm not quite ready," she said as she went to the fridge. "Here's a beer. Go back and get dressed. Give me about five minutes." She gave him a kiss and patted his butt to shoo him away.

She added the finishing touches and then beckoned him. She didn't tell him the entire plan, but he agreed to the premise. She asked him to sit down, removed the scarf from her pocket, and tied it over his eyes. It smelled faintly of her, and he inhaled the scent in anticipation.

First she brought him a glass of red wine, a Duckhorn Decoy pinot noir, pleasant and light—nothing special unless being tasted with a blindfold on and a sexy woman choreographing dinner. She brought the glass to his lips, not wanting him to spill it. He ran his fingers along her legs as he sipped. She moved away and grabbed a piece of tuna, laid it on a slice of mango, and asked him to open wide. He laughed and did as he was told. He groaned with the sheer complexity of taste. Then she delivered a piece of mahi layered on a slice of papaya with a squirt of fresh lime and brought her glass of chardonnay to his lips. He was really enjoying the game and knew exactly where it was headed. The next bite too was delivered with her fingers, but this time he pulled her forefinger into his mouth, sucking the flavor of both the food and her off it before releasing. *That tongue again, hmmm.* She willed her mind back to the food. The wine was right there to punctuate each offering, and it was starting to go to her head.

The wine was beginning to affect Sterling, as well, as she began reminiscing about Clyde, Dags, and her relationships with both. Clyde had personified the fun in dysfunctional. From the outset there were no rules or expectations; everything was very superficial, very light. Such relationships quickly run their course without anyone getting hurt, and so it had with Sterling and Clyde. Clyde and Dags had been like brothers, and the three of them hung out together. In an odd way, it was almost natural for Sterling to gravitate to Dags. During some melodramatic moments, she pictured herself as Katherine Ross with Paul Newman and Robert Redford in *Butch Cassidy and the Sundance Kid*. She smiled at the memory. One of her first books, *Outlaw Passions*, had dealt with that fantasy. She remembered Dags as the more serious of the two, more grounded in life than Clyde—and for that, Clyde had loved him. Except for their mutual rambunctiousness with people and their shared love of drugs, they couldn't have been more different; in hindsight, it was a weird relationship. She wondered what had happened to split them apart. Clyde's funeral was in two days. Would Dags even be there?

Next he heard her cross the room, coming back toward him after a trip to the kitchen to bring him another offering, and he heard a fork or a spoon clink against a plate. She told him he might want to take only a small taste of the next part—a little at a time, she suggested—so he was prepared to burn his mouth on whatever concoction she had cooked up to shock him. Tentatively he extended his tongue, but he couldn't discern the flavor. He really didn't want to burn his mouth on her mystery spice. He tried again and still couldn't identify it. Trying to release himself from that fear, he tasted the morsel with his tongue and felt an electric charge—it was hot, all right, but not the kind of heat he had expected! His lips closed around her skin, her nipple, and he sucked it gently into his mouth. His hand encircled her ribcage, and he pulled her toward him, throwing off the blindfold with a deep groan. The wine, the sun, the temptress antics, and the mystery all combined to make him damned hard! He wanted her, and he could see why she had laid the blanket on the floor. There was no way he could wait long enough to get to the bedroom. They scrambled out of their clothes and madly reached for each other, and then, suddenly, time slowed. As excited as they were, it was as though they were in a movie running in slow motion. They took their time, turning seconds into minutes and minutes into a lifetime. They began to touch, explore, and appreciate as though it were the first time ever. It was always like this for them, and tonight would not disappoint. It didn't matter that their dinner lay largely untouched; they could finish it later. It didn't matter that the candles were the only light except for the reflection of the moon off the rippled water. It didn't matter whether there was an identifiable beginning, middle, or end. All that mattered now was available to them. All that mattered was each other. All that mattered now was touch … and feeling … and love.

Wow, when Sterling wanted to, she could write! She loved it, but she was getting loaded. Tomorrow would tell her if she was good. Hemingway's "Write drunk, edit sober" was often her creed; that was about the only thing they had in common except writing in Florida.

Grabbing the phone, she called her sister in Wilmington, Delaware, to check on the availability of a spare bedroom. She and Bethany had always been close, but as they lived their lives, time seemed to lengthen the intervals between calls. Beth had heard the sad news about Clyde through some mutual friends and had called Sterling immediately. Yes, of course she had room. Would Madeleine be coming? Sterling had confided only in Beth about Maddie's father.

"I never really delved into the details with Maddie," Sterling confessed, "but I think that call now needs to be made."

"Let me know what you're doing. I would love to see my niece. It has been too long!" Bethany replied.

"I'll see how the call goes. Bethany, I never found the courage to tell Maddie the truth about her father. You're the only who knows. I think maybe now is the time to tell the person I should have told first."

With a conflicted "good-bye" to her sister, she hung up, called the airlines, and booked two tickets from Fort Myers to Philadelphia, praying that Madeleine would agree to come.

5

After Katy went to bed, I felt like staying up forever, so I called an old buddy in California, Bobby Davis. Now, Bobby is an old friend of mine in both senses: he's older than I am, and I've known him for nearly thirty years.

I was sitting on the couch, grinding about Clyde when I recalled our mutual friend. Bobby needed to know, and I hoped he could help me understand Clyde's demons.

I had met Bobby through Clyde on Nantucket, during our days at Tufts. Nearly forty years old when we met, he had to be pushing seventy now. Bobby had practiced pharmacology in San Francisco under the expert tutelage of Stanley Owsley, known to his friends as Bear, inspiring Clyde to name his dog Bear and nickname his wife Honey Bear, and to the rest of the hippie world as the man who manufactured 1.25 million hits of the purest LSD known to man, or at least to me. We had always kept in touch, primarily because of Clyde. Bobby eventually used his psychedelic expertise to become a licensed pharmacist. He could unabashedly answer some of my nagging questions about Clyde, and more important, we could bullshit together while mourning an old friend.

I grabbed a beer and a joint, figuring Bobby would already be where I wanted to go even with the time change, and made the call. He answered on the second ring.

"Dude," he mumbled, "How the hell are ya?"

"Not so good, Bobby. Look, I've got some really bad news."

"Clyde?" He always intuited my direction, undoubtedly a result of the psychedelic highway he had helped create decades before.

"Yeah, and I shouldn't be surprised that you know."

"Dags, he is our closest mutual friend. He's fun, and he's crazy. When you say you have really bad news, it points to Clyde. Did he die?

"Yes. Bobby, he shot himself."

"Oh shit. Oh, shit. Oh, shit! I'm so sorry, Dags. What happened? Fuck. Fuck. Fuck." I could hear his labored breathing.

I gave him a sanitized version in order to stay on point, but I did mention Clyde's Percocet addiction. I told him about Clyde's hospitalization a year earlier and asked his opinion.

"Dags, I am intimately familiar with Percocet." His accompanying laugh made me smile and relax as I remembered happier days. "I have studied it, used and abused it, and I have enjoyed it immensely." Another laugh escaped, hinting at pharmacological problems far worse than Clyde's, yet conquered. "Percocet, or its generic equivalent, oxycodone, is a class-two narcotic pain reliever, meaning it has a large potential for abuse compared to other prescription drugs. "Now this is boring, Dags, but it's worth remembering. Oxycodone was developed in Germany in 1916 as a better and safer pain reliever than heroin, which had been banned in 1914. In 1898, Bayer pharmaceutical company had released a potent, morphine-derived cough suppressant called heroin. This led to hundreds of thousands of heroin addicts in the US alone. Hence two German scientists synthesized oxycodone as a supposedly nonaddictive synthetic substitute for narcotics like heroin. As the decades rolled on, more was learned about the addictive nature of oxycodone, and more controls were put in place, culminating in 1970 with its designation as a schedule-two drug by the Federal Controlled Substance Act."

"Christ, you sound like an encyclopedia, Bobby, like you're reading from a manual."

"Photographic memory, courtesy of Bear and his experiments. Call it a perk," he said with a laugh. He was sounding better as he reminisced. "In 1950, Percodan—oxycodone cut with aspirin— became a household name. As early as the sixties, the attorney general here in California was condemning Percodan as a scourge afflicting a third of all the addicts in the state. We were all high on LSD at the time, having figured—correctly, I might add—that our drug was less addictive than Percodan, with fewer side effects—except, of course, for the occasional deluded Superman leap from a bridge or a tall building."

We shared a nostalgic chuckle before he continued.

"Anyway, in 1974, the Food and Drug Administration introduced a new oxycodone product called Percocet, an oxycodone pill cut with acetaminophen. In 1996, Perdue Pharma introduced Oxycontin, oxycodone in its pure form, which was supposed to be a safer drug because of its time-release base that was intended to prevent abuse. Drug users in the rural South began crushing the pills, neutralizing their time-release property and making for an extremely potent and addictive high. It quickly became known as 'hillbilly heroin' and was widely distributed in some southern pain clinics by corrupt doctors. The FDA advisory board is currently recommending that Percocet, Vicodin, and every other combination of acetaminophen and narcotic analgesics be removed from the market because of their contributions to an estimated four hundred acetaminophen deaths each year."

I chimed in. "So I think what you're saying is that Clyde suffered an acetaminophen overdose last year. His brother told me that Joanne got home from work one night and found him unresponsive on their living room floor. She called 911, and Clyde was rushed to the ER in critical condition. The ER staff stabilized him, pumped his stomach, and put him on a ventilator for two weeks. From what you're describing, he was suffering from respiratory depression?"

"Exactly! Dags, I taught you well. You always listened better than most."

"It's beginning to make sense now," I replied, still incredulous that Bobby could retain and regurgitate facts that he had learned years ago.

"Clyde's brother said the first several days were rough, as Clyde had to be strapped down while he was weaned off the drug. He had a harder time being weaned off the ventilator.

"Bobby, apparently Clyde only let his immediate family know the details. He told us he had a persistent case of pneumonia. I wondered about that, since he told me the docs wanted him to give up drinking but smoking was okay. Stupid me. If he didn't want to tell me, that was his prerogative. He must have been embarrassed to show us weakness; I just didn't know why. He refused to discuss it with my brother, Jack, as well. He'd simply cut off any questions with a 'Don't go there.' Bobby, someone should have gone there. Someone should have figured out what was really afflicting him. And that someone should have been me. I was his closest friend."

"Dags, don't beat yourself up. Christ, if I worried about all those fuckwads that took acid and tried to fly from the Golden Gate Bridge, I would have chewed on Clyde's gun a long time ago."

"It's just such a waste, Bobby. I suppose his depression from Percocet abuse was beginning to take hold, and he simply didn't want anyone to know. He had so many friends who could have helped him if he had only confided in us, but none of us ever knew he was depressed until his memorial service."

"Dags, he did it to himself, man. That's the way it is. Sorry to be so harsh, but it sounds like he had a boatload of problems, your perceived abandonment being just one of many. Hey, his suicide sucks, but it got me a call from you, right? From death springs life. Tough introduction, I know, but it is what it is. If a guy is intent on doing himself in, he most likely will succeed. Look, I've gotta go—big day tomorrow. I'm not as young as I once was. Dags, my friend, Clyde introduced us, and Clyde connected us tonight. That can't be all bad. Come visit sometime. I've saved a super-secret stash we can share."

With that old, familiar laugh, he was gone.

He awoke, vaguely remembering how he got there. Vodka, Percocet, who knows, maybe even a Xanax or ten. The sirens, Joanne's scared look, people staring down at him as the ambulance raced to the hospital. A lot of confusion, but somehow he found serenity amid the chaos. Wherever he had been was not so bad, maybe even peaceful. But as he returned to reality, the serenity turned to agitation. He couldn't breathe with a tube down his throat and a mask over his face and the lights from the room blinding him. He felt hot and scared. Claustrophobia followed him everywhere. Couldn't escape it. Couldn't move his arms. More shallow breathing, panic overwhelming him. *What happened?* There's Joanne, saying she loved him and that Bear missed him. There's his brother, wasting his time. *Where's Dad?* Where he'd always been—not there.

He opened his eyes and heard his breath through the oxygen mask. The hollow sound dominated his senses, transforming his entire being into the pumping sound of his mask. He felt like each breath was magnified into a heartbeat, and each beat grew progressively louder as it searched for escape from the mask. When it could grow no louder within, the beat began to circumvent the mask, becoming less personal. The thumping increased, tearing at his ears as it escaped the workings of the mask and began to pervade the entire room. When he could no longer stand it, when he felt his ears beginning to explode, the heartbeat diminished and became more localized, concentrating in a certain area of the room. He tried to pinpoint the location of the sound but could not, until a subtle movement caught his eye. It came from the corner of the room, near the open closet door. He tried to raise his head but couldn't. There it was again, closer this time. An animal, a beastly animal, taking shape in the form of … what? What was it? How did it get in the room? Where were the fucking nurses?

His breathing quickened, and he began to thrash against the restraints as the echoes magnified and the claustrophobia advanced with the beast. Oh god, the beast was a dragon, and with each breath, a blast of fire emanated from its prehistoric mouth. Its rheumy eyes stared right through him as it began to move, languidly at first, surveying its surroundings, alert for danger as it sized up its prey. Oh god! He was the prey. *Please be a nightmare,* he begged as the beast moved closer, confident in the kill. The room began to darken, save the pulsating emissions of fire, as the walls closed in. He tried to ward off the beast but couldn't lift his arms. His pulse raced as its stale breath enveloped him and the fire blew closer, stinging his nostrils with each shallow breath. As the dragon reached for his heart, as the claws began to dig into his chest, he started screaming. He screamed like he never had before and kept screaming long after the nurse came running in.

Then it was gone, fading into the darkness as the light returned. The bright lights burned his eyes as the nurse studied the monitors before looking down.

"It's all right now, Mr. Colson. You just had a bad dream. I am going to administer some antianxiety medication that should make you sleep."

Clyde lay back against the sweat-drenched pillows, his eyes closing as he exhaled into sleep.

He was flying, unencumbered by the shackles of earth, Icarus seeking cosmic freedom. It was dark, cold, like outer space. He was no longer afraid as he flew through galaxies, a human spacecraft rocketing millions of miles in a matter of moments. He had never experienced such freedom as he accelerated past planets that seemed to represent chapters in his life. The first planet held an image of the mother he remembered as a child. She was young, she was beautiful, and she loved him so very much. He felt a surge of that love as he sped by her and raced toward the next planet, his father. He instinctively recoiled when he saw him and veered off course to escape the threat of destruction. He knew he was wrong to fly away, and he yearned for his father's acceptance, so he punched in new coordinates to return. Setting a course for a direct hit, he locked his eyes on the planet that was his father. As he neared the planet, his father relaxed and beckoned him closer, and the promised warmth of paternal love enveloped him. His father loved him. He knew it, and he felt the freedom of happiness as he angled away, exchanging smiles and waves with his father while soaring deeper into space.

He could sense the increase in speed as he flew through the dark void, passing a myriad of stars as he searched for the next planet, his wife. Seeing a bright light ahead, he set his course. There she was, smiling his way. As he closed the distance, tears began to form in his eyes, the friction from his speed constricting them into pulsating, narrow rivulets that ran down his cheeks. She still loved him! He knew it! He could see it in her eyes. His tears became tears of joy as he rushed past her open arms, setting his course for Dagger.

His velocity created a warm whoosh around his body, protecting him from the cold. He believed he was coursing through heaven, as the warmth seemed to be emanating from the hand of God. He had never felt so spiritual as the oncoming stars lay down a path of dominoes to Dagger's planet. He began to orbit as it came into view, shrouded in shadow, visibility near zero. He began to panic, needing to establish a connection before hurtling past. He was beginning to lose sight of it when it rotated. There was Dagger—or was it? The planet was engulfed in dense clouds—the face barely visible, recognition impossible. He turned his head to view the rapidly vanishing planet, his heart sinking as he realized there was no possibility of return.

He adjusted his gaze to the front, his eyes tearing and the warmth of the voyage dissipating. A large planet lay ahead. There was no way to avoid a collision. Rather than turn away, he chose to confront the mayhem. As he flew closer, he noticed a strange woman wearing a nurse's cap. He did not flinch as the woman grew larger and the planet got closer. Closer he came, a crash imminent, the bright planet overwhelming his dark world. The nurse smiled at him as her image grew until his ship and the planet were one and he was peering into her eyes.

Clyde awoke to a chill—the nurse injecting him again—and again he fell back asleep. He had no idea how long he'd been sleeping; it had felt like forever. The rocket ship did not return, and his sleep was dreamless.

Joanne was reading at his bedside when he began to stir. The evidence of the excesses of her marriage—her prematurely lined face and emaciated body—was more pronounced now as Clyde fought his demons. She had been there for most of the week and had witnessed his thrashing as he struggled to regain consciousness.

The doctor had informed her that Clyde had overdosed on the acetaminophen from Percocet as well as Xanax and alcohol, and that he was fortunate to be alive. These nightmares would continue until he was weaned from the drug, hence the injections.

Clyde opened his eyes and saw her but was too weak to talk, so he simply looked. He seemed scared, she thought, so she began to rub his cheek lightly as she talked about anything but his condition.

"Hey there. Are you back in the land of the living?" she asked before realizing she might have sounded a little too flippant.

Clyde looked at her and blinked. He was scared, confused, tired.

"That's okay, dear, save your strength. You've had a tough couple of days. The doctors say you're doing well, and you'll be able to go home as soon as you can breathe on your own. It shouldn't be more than a few days. Are you thirsty?"

He nodded, never relinquishing his frightened expression.

She marked and closed her book, adding, "Here, let me get you some water."

She left the room to find a nurse. Meanwhile Clyde tried to remember what had happened, but he was too tired and weak to concentrate. He shuddered, though, as he remembered the late-night intruder—as if he didn't have enough to worry about without another hallucinogenic nightmare penetrating his soul. Did he fly through space to escape the dragon or simply to escape?

Joanne returned with a nurse who was carrying a pitcher and a cup of water that was mostly crushed ice.

"Mr. Colson, I am going to remove your mask for a moment and give you a sip of water. Would you like that?"

Clyde nodded. His throat felt as hot as that damned intruder's breath. Did the dragon visit him last night or the night before, or had it been every night?

He turned to the nurse and croaked, "How long have I been here?" He was barely able to form the question because his throat was so dry.

"You have been with us for a week. You look so much stronger now. Here, let's cool your throat with some ice. Not too much at first," she gently warned as she carefully placed half a teaspoon into his mouth. He closed it, savoring the moisture and the chill, and began feeling better. After a few moments she gave him another small helping and then placed the mask back on his face.

He pushed it away. "Can I leave it off so I can talk with my wife?"

"Please, Mr. Colson, only for a couple of minutes," the nurse said, glancing at Joanne.

"Thank you, I'll replace it soon," Joanne replied as she filled the cup with more water. "Here, hon, drink this."

She brought the cup to his lips, and as the nurse left, Clyde grasped his wife's hand. "Joanne, I'm so sorry for doing this to you. I don't know what I would do without you." He looked away, fighting back tears.

Joanne pulled him close. "I love you," she whispered. "We'll get through this together." She pulled him closer, willing his demons away. "Your Honey Bear is here."

Clyde gently pushed away. He squeezed her hand and said, "I'm so embarrassed about this, putting everyone through this. Has my father been by? Who knows about this?"

"No, your dad hasn't been by, but I've been talking with him nightly," she lied. "He's very concerned and said to take as much time as you need to get well. Pete has been by to see you, but I haven't told anyone else. Oh, and your brother dropped in while you were sleeping."

"I don't want anyone to know, especially Dagger and Jack. I'll tell them something when the time comes."

He was suddenly feeling tired. Joanne brought the cup to his lips for a final sip before replacing the mask.

"Honey, you sleep. I'll be right here if you need me."

Joanne bent down to give him a kiss and returned to her chair and her book, trying not to cry. She had never seen him like this before. With all the partying they had done, she had never expected it to get this far out of hand. He had always been so strong. Now he was about to die. He looked so weak, so vulnerable, lying there barely able to breathe, struggling to stay alive. How could she survive without him? Frightened, she reached down and grasped his hand. She pulled it toward her and gently laid her forehead against his wrist, praying that he would never leave her. Clyde slept, unaware of her plea as he unconsciously awaited the return of his nighttime visitor.

I awoke the next morning feeling the way I should have expected to feel after the events of the previous day (receiving Clyde's virulent phone call, finding his body, and consuming enough alcohol to begin to cross the bridge past that tragedy): dazed, confused, and hung over. Katy was already up and quite obviously still pissed. I couldn't blame her. I was attempting to put a positive spin on the call and coming up short. As much as I wanted to quickly dismiss it as eternal, angry payback, I needed to try to paint it more sympathetically, primarily for my own protection. Katy was more pragmatic, refusing to believe anything other than the obvious: Clyde had tried to take me down with him. She couldn't reconcile his last moments enough to attend his service—basically her attitude was "He can rot in hell. That's my baby."

I had more of a dilemma to contend with. Clyde had been a very close friend, and his wife held me directly responsible for his suicide. There was no getting around that. If she saw me there, no telling what she would do. The last thing I wanted was a scene. My brother would be giving one of the eulogies, having grown close to Clyde over the years of my friendship with him; yet over the last nine months, Clyde had spurned that closeness too. Jack occasionally called him, but Clyde never answered and never returned his messages. Jack just figured Clyde was in one of his "Fuck Dagger" funks and would eventually get over it.

I wanted to hear Jack speak. I needed to hear him speak. He still possessed the beauty of Clyde's soul within him—something I no longer had.

I grabbed a cup of coffee and walked outside, hoping a shot of fresh spring air might ameliorate my depression. My thoughts wandered back to Clyde.

At the time of our estrangement, a pissed-off Clyde had gone to Jack, saying that I was dead to him because of my betrayal of him to his family. Jack was stuck between a rock and a hard place; his close friend hated his brother. Jack loved partying with Clyde but realized that Clyde needed to dry out, at least partially—that is, go to rehab for the meds without worrying about the alcohol. We all knew he was too addicted to give up everything, but giving up the meds might save his life. So Jack had used all his diplomatic skills to soften the situation while steering Clyde toward a temporary break from his many abuses. It almost worked. Time after time Jack would call me, saying he thought Clyde might go to rehab, and time after time Clyde would return to his old bullheaded self and refuse, most likely for a couple of reasons—a healthy dose of anger at his father, and a dash of Pete and Joanne saying he really didn't need to go.

Clyde's dysfunctional relationship with his family was interesting, to put it mildly. Now, I know we all come from families with various forms of dysfunction, but his family was so fucked up that an enterprising producer could make a TV series based on them. When I met the oldest brother—now estranged from his family, as well—he accused me of cheating at poker. Getting four of a kind twice in an hour usually does that if you're not among friends. Clyde promptly took him out back and beat the shit out of him. I don't think I've seen the guy since. That was Clyde's first expression of loyalty to me, and I knew he would always protect me after he attacked one of his own. I was never able to match that loyalty, and I've only recently begun to understand his obsessive love for me and everyone connected to me.

His father ran the business that his maternal grandfather had started. In short, Clyde's mother's father let the new son-in-law into the family business. He didn't earn it; he was just lucky enough to marry into it—a gift, so to speak, but a gift that left him with the company after the patriarch's death.

Now the "good," younger son, the most dispassionate man you could ever meet, did everything right and joined the company after graduating from college—another gift.

Clyde was a different story. Because of a few screwups in college, most involving me as a willing participant, his father made him jump through a lot of hoops before he was even considered for a position in the company. When his father finally accepted him, he did so with many strings attached. That never sat well with Clyde, who resented it from the day he started until the day he died. Not only did he work for a father who'd never accepted him for who he was, but he also worked for the younger brother he'd never liked.

Eventually the time came when Clyde's father, after talking with me, decided that Clyde needed to jump through another hoop, and Clyde, ornery as ever and saddled with an addiction that obviously affected his judgment, was finally sick and tired of his father's demands. He also knew he had been entitled working at the company and yearned to spread his wings and finally do something on his own. The problem with that was, again, his drug addiction.

I knew Clyde was a very intelligent man. I knew he was self-sufficient, and I knew he was a survivor. Had he only been able to slay the dragon, he would have not only survived, but thrived in whatever he wanted to do.

A passing robin, the first I had seen this spring, diverted my thoughts from Clyde's death, prompting me to decide to attend the memorial service. Clyde had been a popular guy, so the church was going to be filled. Having been to Christ Church before, I knew there were plenty of places in the back or in the balcony where I could hide. Maybe I could sneak in as the service was about to start, and be the first to leave. Yes, I've always been good at covering my ass.

I found Katy at her computer and related my decision to her. She gave me a cursory, pissed-off glance and said, "Do what you gotta do and don't cause a scene."

I thanked her for those nurturing words and returned to my reminiscence.

Pete Everhart had been Clyde's oldest friend, a friend since childhood. I didn't know him well because I didn't want to get to know him well after our introduction. You might be getting the picture that I'm a hard-ass. I am. If something or someone doesn't sit right with me, then I really never warm up to that situation or person. Pete was one of those people. He had a mean streak that bordered on evil and a cynicism that made me uncomfortable, but Clyde and Pete had grown up together, and a bond like that was hard to break, so I kept my distance. Pete had suffered through a couple of broken marriages and a daughter's suicide. Dirty blond hair, balding, with a natural, sinister glare, if he was jaded when I met him as a single man with no children, you can imagine what he was like now.

I soon discovered that their bond extended to Percocet; Pete was Clyde's vehicle to the pain management doctor. Once that happened, Pete had a new playmate, a buddy from his past who could temporarily change his dark world into a euphoric garden.

Joanne and Clyde had married relatively late in life, a marriage blended with alcohol and drug abuse. At their wedding, Pete had laughed at the concept of their having children, saying it would be a payback to the world if they did. Great friend, great comment.

I never saw Joanne at a party where she didn't fall down, and after they were married, I could say the same about Clyde. Toward the end, they began falling down together, a drunken duet. His Percocet addiction was making him sloppy and not much fun to be around. I began to pull back.

I began nitpicking his faults and weaknesses instead of championing his assets. I now realize that we are all obviously human, with a cluster of warts that sometimes obscures our wonderful traits. Clyde had an abundance of both, and that is why I needed to go to his service. I needed a dose of the old Clyde. I needed to listen to my brother tell me why I used to love him, and how I needed to rekindle that love in order to survive myself.

How had Clyde reached this precipice of life and decided to jump? An insatiable love of drugs and alcohol was the simple answer, but many of us share this love and manage not to self-destruct. In one of my conversations with his father, he said that Clyde's DNA contributed to his alcoholism. Clyde's maternal side was rife with alcoholics, including his mother, her brothers, and her father, as well as his older brother and younger sister. The only one spared was that dispassionate brother. Sometimes I felt he should drink more in order to become more human, when actually he needed to exert complete control over himself in order not to fall. He was lucky, if that's what you want to call it, because his DNA came mostly from his father, leading to their partnership in business as well as human relations.

The few times I was with Clyde's family, the absence of love among them was obvious. His relationship with his mother was one I never figured out because she died before I got the chance to know her. My recollection was of a stern woman who could no longer enjoy herself because she couldn't escape her life without alcohol, so she channeled her energy into a dutiful life devoted to raising a family and supporting charitable causes. I never saw her smile, but Clyde's friends, myself included, were so nervous around her that we created uncomfortable situations that later made us laugh.

The first time I met her was at her formal dinner table when I was in my twenties and stoned most of the time, including that night. Clyde's father was still at work, so the dinner included Clyde, another buddy, and me. We had just taken our seats in her dark, forbidding formal dining room, and I had the seat of honor to her left. Lucky me. The guys were very nervous and, again, very stoned and hoping to eat quickly and escape unscathed. That prayer went out the window within the first few minutes of dinner. I hadn't even taken a bite when I began to pour myself some iced tea from a pitcher. The ice clogged the spout as I was pouring, and so I tipped the pitcher more steeply. That was a bad move. A cascade of ice broke the dam, filling my glass with tea and ice, which then overflowed onto my fancy dinner plate of untouched chicken and vegetables. Clyde's mother shot daggers at Dagger. First impressions are very important, so until her death several years later, I tried to forestall the second impression for as long as I could.

The funniest story involving Clyde, his mother, and his friends also took place at a dinner table, but this time the locale was a fancy restaurant celebrating something I've long forgotten. I laugh because I was absent, adhering to that second-impression delay. This time one of Clyde's other friends occupied the dubious seat of honor; he was well versed in the art of polite, drunken conversation—or so he thought. Clyde was busy with his own drunken conversation when his mother snapped his name. He looked over and saw a very pissed-off woman demanding that he help remove his friend's head from the mashed potatoes and then remove his friend from the restaurant. I believe this singular event either elevated my status in her eyes simply because of my absence, or else lumped us all together as "my wasted son's wasted friends." Hey, at least I never passed out in a plate of mashed potatoes.

I always believed Clyde's father really enjoyed my company as well as the company of Clyde's other buddies. As much as I enjoyed his company, though, I never saw him as a nurturing father. I saw him as a cool father, a guy who could gamble with us, play golf with us, and relate to us on our level.

Shortly after Clyde graduated from college, his father offered to take him and a friend to Las Vegas as a graduation present. That friend turned out to be me. How could I not think the man was cool? I was an impressionable twenty-three-year-old guy who loved to gamble, and here was my buddy's father taking me to the gilded palace of sin. His father showed us the high roller side of Las Vegas: we dined at fine restaurants, played golf at the Dunes, and watched him glide through the casinos in all his sophistication. Back then I wished my father was that suave. What the hell did I know?

One night Clyde and I were licking our wounds over dinner as we related stories of our blackjack losses that day. We were virtually broke, with two nights left to gamble. How could we survive? Clyde's father had the answer. He taught us the "don't pass" theory of craps—the theory being that rollers betting the pass line rarely make three consecutive passes. Either a seven ruins their number, or they roll craps right away. Now, if a roller succeeds in making three passes, he is hot and should be avoided. According to the theory, you should bet five dollars, and if you lose, you should double the bet to ten dollars, and if you lose that, double the bet to twenty. You will win one of those three passes.

We began to win, and by the end of the night we had each made a hundred dollars, or twenty units. The drawback is the negative energy you exude at a table where people are betting to win lots of numbers. When you win the don't pass line, nobody likes you. There is no camaraderie with the rest of the table. It's a grinding way to make money. It's work.

With that in mind, Clyde and I, being brilliant college graduates, quickly decided that we could move to Las Vegas and make thirty thousand dollars a year playing craps. We floated the idea by his father the following night at dinner, curious about his opinion. Years later he was still relating the story to friends who became part of our annual pilgrimage to Las Vegas. The story became legendary with each recounting, as he regaled them with the details of his belly laugh over the seriousness of our proposition. He said he had never heard anything funnier.

For Clyde and me, the Las Vegas trip helped cement a friendship that began our freshman year at Tufts, a liberal arts university in Medford, Massachusetts. We were both underachievers who had attended prep school and then chosen a second-tier university because the top tier saw right through us. Tufts didn't care about that as long as our parents paid the exorbitant tuition. And they did.

Shortly after I arrived at my final stop of higher learning, I discovered the economic benefit of importing hashish from Switzerland hidden in cuckoo clocks. The quality of the hash earned me a reputation that I somehow thought was beneficial at the time.

Clyde lived down the hill from me in a different section of campus. He was selling cocaine when he heard about a guy with Afghan gold seal hash that had been imported in cuckoo clocks from Switzerland.

One day he paid me a visit. We were nineteen years old, and our parents were losing the drug war against us. We had no choice but to unite in our fight. And fight we did. We took the war to San Juan, Puerto Rico, and Saint John in the American Virgin Islands, and as far west as Las Vegas. We became fast friends, and that friendship endured for thirty years. As I said, our friendship was born from drugs and died from drugs. In between there were too many stories to tell—some funny, some tragic, but all memorable.

8

Boca Grande, Florida, is an enclave of the rich who try to avoid being famous. In the late 1800s, the area itself became famous as a major deepwater port for the shipment of phosphate. Thus was born the village of Boca Grande. A railroad was soon constructed on Gasparilla Island, extending south to where a state-of-the-art port operated, continuously loading barges with phosphate to be delivered around the world.

At about the same time, wealthy sportsmen discovered the abundance of tarpon during their spring run, and fishing became the primary reason for the evolution of Boca Grande into what it is today. Many wealthy northerners bought land and built winter residences there. Eventually the phosphate companies found more convenient ports for shipping, and so tarpon fishing and tourism became vital to the town's economic survival. Many of these wealthy northerners lived in Wilmington, Delaware, and were part of the Du Pont family ; they often referred to Boca Grande as "Wilmington South." Throughout the month of March, trains from the north would be full of families escaping for a few weeks to some southern paradise. The train leaving Tampa, that had begun as passenger train, would evolve into a freight train carrying phosphate to the Boca Grande port with only a couple of passenger cars of vacationers left for Boca Grande . These passengers would disembark in Boca Grande and walk to their houses as the train continued south to the port. The train was discontinued in 1959, by which time it had become more convenient to fly to Tampa and drive from there.

It was during a March vacation in the 1970s that Sterling Rodgers discovered the beauty of Boca Grande. She was not part of the Du Pont family, but she had many friends who were, and for a couple of years she accompanied a wealthy girlfriend and her family to the island. It was love at first sight for the middle-class girl as she witnessed the serenity of the small beach community.

When Dags Bissell pulled his Houdini act and disappeared, a devastated Sterling did the same, moving to Boca Grande as a soon-to-be single mother. She rented a room in a cottage and found a job proofreading for another aspiring writer, making enough money to coast through the summer writing her first novella and raising her newborn daughter, Madeleine. She sent the manuscript to a publisher she had met the previous winter; he'd seen promise in the attractive author—maybe more in the girl than in the writer. She signed a modest contract to write a book, beginning with the expansion of her novella. By the following spring, she was locally famous as the pretty lady writer who lived alone. The publisher got his wish of having an affair with Sterling, and Sterling got her wish of having her book published. After two years of freelance writing and getting profits from the book, she bought a small cottage in Boca Grande and began calling it home.

As Madeleine grew, more books followed, each more successful than the previous one, while Sterling perfected the art of the romance novel.

Sterling suddenly realized she had been swinging the black pump on her right toe for the last five minutes, deep in thought—or, more accurately, zoned out. She had begun organizing her clothes for the trip while putting off making the phone call to Madeleine, when she had simply stopped and sat down midstream—knees crossed, wearing a bra and panties—without even feeling like getting the rest of the way dressed.

Memorial services were not her thing. It wasn't that she didn't want to honor the person or acknowledge his life and death; she simply felt uncomfortable being in church for such an occasion, especially this church and this occasion. She knew that everybody felt that way, but this would be a little different. It would be Clyde's day, but Dags would probably be there, and his presence would throw open the door to a past that she thought she had permanently closed years ago.

What do you do when you see the unsuspecting father of your child, and that child, now a twenty-three-year-old woman, is standing at your side? Overwhelmed by the enormity of the situation, Sterling began second-guessing her decision to go to the service and finally open up to Madeleine. She had spent much of the day wrestling with this conundrum and had revisited her past novels to glean an answer. Parts of her life and sometimes the life she imagined Dags to be leading, were interwoven into many of her stories, but "Hanging on the Moon" gave her the conviction she needed to unlock her past. The story described the secret love between a young servant and the married man of the manor. The servant became pregnant and ran away in shame to protect the father, only to learn years later that his wife had died and he had become a shell of a man. She found the courage to return to his house and discovered that he had been searching for her, his only true love, since his wife's death. Haltingly she told him of his son, by then a young man and the spitting image of his father. Their love affair reignited, and they all lived happily ever after.

Sterling had tried her hand at tragic endings, but they always made her too sad for too long. She was a true romantic at heart.

Now she knew what she needed to do, but would Dags even be there? He had been Clyde's best friend, but she had heard a rumor of their falling out with Clyde's parting shot—verbal, that is. (She let out a dark laugh at her witticism and made a mental note to use that phrase in a future manuscript.) Dags probably blamed himself, even if everyone on earth knew he was simply the last scapegoat for Clyde's excesses and excuses. Funny how when someone finally gives up and does himself in, people tend to forgive him a little more.

When or if she saw Dags, Sterling would have a couple of choices to make. If he looked right through her or showed superficial interest, she would tamp down her emotions and simply walk away, hiding the tears she knew would soon flow. But if he exhibited the kindness and sincerity that she believed he possessed, then somehow she needed to find the words to introduce him to their daughter. The next move would be his.

Her mind drifted back to what she should wear. She knew she should be as inconspicuous as possible, with black being the most appropriate color. She preferred navy, though, and selected a couple of outfits, alternately holding each one up against her body as she looked in the mirror. She began to examine herself. The past twenty-four years had been kind; she was lucky. She had just turned fifty, but her facial wrinkles still resembled laugh lines, she'd colored her hair only slightly to maintain some blond from her youth, and her figure had gotten a little fuller but not more than the natural aging process demanded. She wanted to look good if she saw him but not over the top, so she chose a conservative navy-blue dress, a string of pearls to wear around her neck, and a pair of navy flats instead of the pumps. Beth had said the weather would be nice—spring attempting an early entrance—so she selected a burgundy wool overcoat to complete the look. Too much navy? Too aggressive with the burgundy? She had other things to think about.

Why had he left? She had been so in love with him. Why the hell had he left? She surprised herself with this sudden intrusion of anger. She bit her clenched fist and then began to cry—quietly at first, but reaching a crescendo that she had repressed for many years. Every child needs two parents, and she had purposefully deprived Maddie of the chance to have a relationship with her father, the man who helped create her and who was about to reappear after twenty-four years.

She had tried to be honest with her daughter, offering a sanitized version of her relationship with Dags but never revealing the genuine sorrow she still felt from the loss. She had been working in a bookstore in Wilmington when he came sauntering in. She had recently parted ways with Clyde, and Dags knew it, so he easily found her. They began with a couple of lunches, and then there was that friendly dinner with too many drinks that led to her bed. She distinctly remembered falling for him the day he walked into the store and said hi, but after that surprisingly intimate night, she began to pull away. She didn't want to appear overly excited about him lest he treat her like just another conquest. After a couple of weeks of some healthy pleading from him, though, she finally agreed to see him again, and so began her magical love affair with the young man of her dreams. She didn't know it then, but she had been born to write sappy novels, in spite of her rock 'n' roll roots.

She let out a sigh and was about to pick up the phone to call Madeleine when it suddenly rang. It was her daughter. They spoke nearly every day.

"Hi Mom. Are you busy packing?" Maddie already knew the answer was yes.

"Yes, dear, just picking out something appropriate. That's funny, I was just about to call you," Sterling replied anxiously, knowing it was time for that talk. She began absentmindedly twirling her hair, an annoying habit she exhibited when she was distracted, confused, or upset.

"Mom, I can almost hear you twirling your hair. Have you been crying? You sound congested. What's up?"

"I don't know. I don't like funerals, I guess, especially this one. And I hate to fly." She walked to the fridge and grabbed a bottle of water. She also spied a bottle of wine, a much better idea, so she replaced the water with the wine, something she liked to sip while chatting with her daughter. She got a glass and poured herself some to take the edge off, leaving the bottle within arm's reach.

"Mom, are you listening to me?" Again, Maddie already knew the answer.

"I'm sorry, dear; the last couple of days have been very distracting. What were you saying?"

"I was just telling you about the cool concert I went to last night in Tampa. We saw the Killers. Wow! What a show!"

The Killers—nice name for a band. And she had to tell me now, Sterling mused. This was turning out to be a disjointed phone call at a time when she needed some clarity and focus. She took a sip. "Honey, we need to talk about this. It's quite upsetting to me."

Madeleine cut her off. "Mom, I know this guy was an old friend of yours, but you hadn't really kept in touch. And he killed himself. He didn't want to live. Just go, pay your respects, and leave. It won't be as bad as you're making it out to be. You'll be all right."

"It's a little more complicated than that, Madeleine," Sterling replied, not doing a very good job at disguising her exasperation. "People don't kill themselves simply because they don't want to live. Many reach a point where they feel they must die to escape pain or depression or loss. Many, if not all, suicide victims want to live, but their life circumstances won't allow it, so they feel the only way out is to murder themselves. But enough of that. There is something else I need to tell you, something I should have told you a long time ago." Sterling took a generous sip of wine and continued. "Your father may be there."

There was a long pause on the other end.

"Maddie, are you still there?"

Mother and daughter had formed such a tight-knit bond over the years that Madeleine had never really missed having a father. Her mother was everything to her, and so hearing that revelation now caught the normally loquacious girl by surprise.

"What? My father's going to be there?" she asked, her voice beginning to quaver.

"Yes."

"The guy who walked out on you may be there?" she continued, gaining strength.

"Madeleine, please. That was a long time ago."

"Mom, you don't have to speak with him or even see him if you don't want to. He's a jerk. What happened between you happened a long time ago. Anyway, he's probably married—and bald and fat, as he should be for treating you like that." A quiet giggle nearly escaped Sterling. "Look Mom, I don't need to know a guy who treated my mother like he treated you. Please don't feel like you need to do something extreme because of me."

"Madeleine"—Sterling struggled to find the right words—"I haven't been entirely honest with you." She intensified her hair twirling, which now bordered on clumsy extraction. "Your father and I had a more serious relationship than I ever let on. I was desperately in love with him when he left, and the last couple of days have brought some old emotions back to the surface. I don't think I ever resolved my feelings about him, even though I hated him for leaving. He never told me why, and we never spoke again." She paused and took a slow breath. "He doesn't know about you. I wrote him a letter that I gave to his parents, but he never responded. I didn't tell him I was pregnant because I wanted him to return out of love, not duty." There was another pause on the other end as Madeleine digested this information.

"Maddie, I know you must be really upset with me. I lied to you. I can't believe I did that."

Sterling's voice cracked as she struggled to continue. "Please forgive me, Madeleine. I've been a terrible mother to you by withholding this truth."

Madeleine began weeping softly. "Mommy, you're my whole world. Don't you know that by now? You gave up so much to raise me by yourself. You have been a remarkable mother, and you are my closest friend. I don't want you to feel guilty about anything you have said or done to me. Hey, maybe he still loves you."

"Honey," Sterling said, regaining some control, "that only happens in my books, not in real life. But if he is there, I hope I can find the time and the courage to talk with him, and I hope he finds the same courage to listen. I want him to know about the precious gem we created together, and someday I want you to meet him."

"Mom, would you like me to go with you? I can be packed in an hour, and I'll drive down. We can go out to dinner, watch the sunset, and have a slumber party like the old days. That would be fun! If I meet him, you don't have to introduce me as his daughter—just as *your* daughter. We can let the rest take care of itself." Madeleine didn't know why she made the offer, but it seemed so right.

"Honey, how did I get so blessed with such a beautiful, mature, and loving daughter? I love you so much, and I am so touched. I was secretly hoping you might want to come after you heard my tear-jerking story, so I bought two tickets, just in case. Oh, and we're staying with Aunt Bethany. She will be so excited when I tell her you're coming!"

Mother and daughter exchanged teary laughs and I love yous before saying good-bye.

When Sterling hung up the phone, it seemed like a great weight had been lifted from her shoulders. Madeleine's offer to accompany her to Wilmington put a completely different spin on her emotions. No longer was she facing a memorial service alone. No longer was she dreading a chance meeting with a long-lost love. Now she had Madeleine to offer encouragement and strength during a difficult time. By the end of their trip, many of her repressed emotions would be resolved. She couldn't wait!

What a fool I was not to have confronted this earlier, she chastised herself. This trip had evolved into an adventure, with so many possibilities to explore—and she'd be exploring them all with her daughter by her side. Excited, she called Hudson's, the local market, to see what kind of fresh catch the fishermen had delivered. The butcher said the boat would be in at 3:00 p.m. with swordfish and grouper. She reserved some grouper and then resumed packing with a decidedly different air about her.

"Pete. Pete. It's Joanne," she cried into the phone. "Clyde's about to stick a shotgun in his mouth. Please come, Pete, please!"

Pete could hear her pleading with Clyde to put the gun away. "I'll be right over," he replied. "Try to calm him down, and tell him you love him and will help him." He hung up, grabbed his coat, took a deep, calming breath, and headed for the car, muttering, "Shit," under his breath. It was Valentine's Day.

He lit a cigarette as he got in the car. He was intimately acquainted with this program. He had detoxed from Percocet six months earlier, and it had been the greatest fight of his life. His doctor, Merlin Sanders, an old family friend, had begun prescribing Percocet for him, as well as Xanax and Ambien, after the death of his daughter, Caitlin. The Everhart family had a history of depression that had cursed Pete's mother and Pete, as well as Caitlin. But her depression was especially insidious, as it had manifested itself when she was a young teenager, and a team of doctors had been unable to find the appropriate cocktail to temper her mood swings. The depression worsened as she got older. After a night of drinking and a run-of-the-mill argument with some of her freshman sorority sisters, she had gone racing off in her BMW and was killed in a head-on with an old oak tree—a fatal accident for the statisticians, but a suicide for all intents and purposes. Pete had gone off the deep end, and Sanders had come running.

He took another drag of his Pall Mall as he relived his own battle with the dragon.

Years of abuse had found him lying in a hospital bed—strapped down, salivating, convulsing, wanting to die. The first wave came and went, leaving him drenched in sweat. Time to rest: try to breathe, relax, hope it doesn't return. He knew it would, and it did with a vengeance, barreling toward him like a thundering runaway locomotive. Another trip to the fires of hell: headaches like you wouldn't believe, convulsions, hallucinations. Death would have been a welcome relief at that point. Again the convulsions subsided, but Pete knew they'd return, felt his entire body stiffen as he spied the hallucinogenic form of that fire-breathing dragon. He knew the dragon was coming, but he was powerless to stop it. He was breathless, with cold sweats. *Here it comes.* The fear itself was enough to kill him. *Gotta keep fighting. Dragon gets you if you die.* He willed the dragon away for the time being, relaxing his body to ease the pain from the restraints. He needed 24/7 care to keep him from choking on vomit.

He came to after a week. Where was he? Where'd he been? To hell and back, that's where. Finally untethered, he was placed in a suicide-safe room so he couldn't hurt himself. The nausea, the diarrhea, the sweating—no end in sight, no relief. *Take me, kill me, release me from this hell. Help me!*

He remembered little from the first couple of weeks, but when he began to regain a semblance of control over his life, he knew he needed to make changes. No more play time with Clyde. He cut him off as fast as he could, for self-preservation.

Now Clyde needed his old friend's help, and he needed it badly if he was to survive. As Pete raced up the Colsons' driveway and parked next to the front door, he tried to figure out a way to convince Clyde to get help. He inhaled another long, slow drag to calm down and knocked on the door before entering. When he walked into the house, he saw a pale, sweating shell of the man he had known for forty-five years. That man was sucking on the barrel of a 12-gauge shotgun. If he pulled the trigger ... *Christ! Don't even think about that.*

"Hey Clyde, man," Pete began, searching for calm but finding only turmoil and fear, "how about we talk about this? You don't need to do this. What are you thinking? Come on." He slowly sat down in the nearest chair and lit up another cigarette, offering one to Clyde, who ignored him. He gazed sympathetically at his friend for a few moments before continuing. "You're my best bud. Joanne loves you, can't live without you, and Bear needs you too. What are you doin'? Why are you acting like this toward people who love you? You're stronger than this."

Joanne chimed in. "Honey, I love you so much. Please don't do this to me. I know we can get through this together, you and me. I know we can. Come on, let's give it another try. We want you here with us. Please, baby. Give me the gun."

They don't know how the fuck I feel. They don't know how much I hate them for their arrogance in assuming what I think. Nothin' but two-faced bastards.

He held his breath.

Should I do it now?

Can I pull the trigger?

He took a deep breath, closed his eyes, and visualized the back of his head vacant, free of pain. Enticing, easy—what release.

Bear distracted him. He barked, his stare penetrating Clyde's.

Look at those eyes. He's looking at me. My friend.

I love you, Bear, my only friend, my only companion. Do you understand? Do you know why? You're the only one who really cares.

He began to cry as the walls closed in, the barrel penetrating his throat, searching for purchase.

He gagged.

Slowly he removed the barrel from his mouth, and immediately he began hyperventilating and shaking. "I can't go on like this," he panted. "Everything is crashing down around me. I can't breathe, I can't sleep, I can't live. I have to die. I can't stand this." He began to cry as he placed the gun back in his mouth.

Joanne ran to him and collapsed around him, hugging his knees. "Please, baby, give me the gun," she pleaded, bursting into tears.

Pete slowly made his way over to his friend and put his arm around him. *Shit, if he pulls the trigger now ... dammit, don't think about that!*

"Come on, Clyde, give me the gun. Give it to me, buddy. That's it. That's it."

He began to breathe as Clyde again removed the barrel from his mouth and collapsed to the floor, crying uncontrollably. Pete gently took the gun, lay down with them, and held them both.

After a few minutes, they sat up, Joanne still caressing Clyde, repeating that everything would be all right. Even Bear came over and lay down next to Clyde, forcing his nose under Clyde's forearm for a pat. Clyde began talking to Bear as though the two of them were the only ones in the room.

Pete went to the kitchen to get a bottle of water for himself and a glass of wine for Joanne. On his way back, he stopped at the bar and poured a glass of vodka for Clyde, grabbing the bottle as an afterthought, and brought it back with him. They drank and drank some more. A couple of shots of vodka and Bear's insistent demands seemed to calm Clyde down. His breathing became softer, and the sense of urgency eased. Clyde looked over at Joanne and with a tremor in his voice said, "I don't know if I can keep going like this. Life is too hard for me now. I've got nothing left. I'm so cooked."

Joanne nuzzled closer to him and whispered, "You've got us, honey. Everyone in this room loves you and needs you alive. Please don't leave us." She kissed his neck and pulled his head to her shoulder, cooing, "You will always be your Honey Bear's valentine." All Clyde could do was slowly blink his glazed eyes and sigh.

Pete needed to get home. The night's demands had drawn him back to his own fight and had challenged his fragile sobriety. He moved around the house, going from room to room looking for any weapons that might bring some harm to Clyde. A .22 pistol was the only other gun he found. He neglected to take the rifle mounted above the fireplace like a trophy. Assuming it was too old to fire, he left it. He approached Clyde and Joanne, now sitting on the couch, and looked at his friend. He sat down with them and said, "Clyde, why don't you get some help? Get detoxed, go to camp, get clean, then come back home. It's the only way." He put his hand on Clyde's knee. "Look at me, Clyde." Clyde met his eyes. "I did it, and it was the hardest thing I've ever done, but I did it, and I know you can too. You were always stronger than I've ever been. I know you can do it. Joanne and I will be there for you every step of the way." He paused a moment. "Look, I need to get home, and the two of you need some rest. Call me if you need me. Okay?"

They nodded. "Thanks, Pete," Clyde quietly replied. "I'm fine now. Thanks."

Pete turned and left. He never saw his old friend again.

Joanne and Clyde were alone, Joanne stroking Clyde's neck while Bear lay nearby. "Baby, let's try to get you clean," she whispered. "This shit is killing you, it's killing me, and it's ruining our marriage. I don't know how much more of this I can take."

She wondered how their lives had gotten so out of control these last several years, to where she found herself begging her husband to remove a loaded shotgun from his mouth. She was convinced it was Dags who was at the root of their troubles. She could still remember the day she returned home from work to learn that Dags had told Clyde's family about his drug use. She gave Clyde an unconscious hug, remembering how confused and betrayed he had initially felt. But as he was prone to do, he picked himself up from the ground and bulled forward, turning his love for Dags into a visceral hatred. A week later, his brother and father joined Dags in the "dead to me" category.

She had never really liked Dags—or Dagger, as Clyde had affectionately called him—partly because he never warmed to her. They both knew it, but she realized Clyde loved him, so she kept her concerns to herself. She knew Katy and Dags were still pissed about Clyde's open use of Percocet at Dags's birthday party a few years earlier. Dags had sent Clyde an embarrassing photo of him that no

58

good friend would have sent. Clyde hated being smacked down by Dags, and that photo had done the trick, along with the warning to leave the drugs at home the next time they met. Joanne had warned Clyde that Dags would hurt him again one day, but Clyde wouldn't listen. He was so damned loyal—and look where that loyalty got him. Fortunately, he had finally taken her advice and repudiated their friendship after Dags's phone call.

Having restored some of his strength, and with it some attitude, Clyde replied, "Leave if you want. Everybody else has. But Bear stays." Bear was Clyde's only source of happiness these days. Everything else about his life sucked.

"Don't talk like that," Joanne countered. "I'm not threatening to leave. I just want more of a normal life again, that's all." But she had threatened to leave, at least a few times over the last several weeks, though it was mainly to get his attention.

The past several months had taken an emotional toll on Joanne as she watched her husband spiral out of control. When he was working, Clyde had a purpose in life that got him out of the house Monday through Friday. Joanne was always late getting home from her job, so their interaction was limited to nights and weekends, when painkillers and alcohol were their primary form of recreation.

When Clyde told Joanne of his discussion with his father and brother about his drug use and the resulting parameters, she hadn't known how to react. Should she subtly side with them in order to get Clyde the help she now realized he needed? If she did, her own recreational drug use would effectively cease; she too relied on Clyde's painkillers and occasionally asked Merlin Sanders for a prescription. Could she adapt to such a lifestyle change? Could she handle life if Clyde chose rehab, and would it demand that she check into rehab with him? She was afraid and didn't think she could do it. Or should she counsel Clyde to free himself from his father's bullying grasp? If she followed that route, would she be doing it for Clyde's benefit or because she was afraid to change her own lifestyle? The importance of this decision was not lost on her, but in the end, she did what she had always unconsciously known she would do—nothing.

Joanne had been frightened to see how Clyde would react to his father's ultimatum. His father was both frustrated and angry with the son he could never control; try as he might, he could not convince Clyde to give up his life of abuse. After Clyde's overdose the previous year, he felt like he had done all he could, as both a father and a boss, by allowing Clyde to take whatever steps were necessary to get well. After the phone call from Dags, he realized those efforts had all been for naught. Hence he gave Clyde the ultimatum: get help now or leave the company. Frankly, he was too old and tired to continue babysitting his son; he felt it was time for Clyde to finally accept some responsibility for his actions. Joanne knew this, having always sensed the friction between Clyde and his father. Ultimately she let Clyde make his own decision, saying she would support whatever choice he made. When he chose to leave the company, it initially seemed like a great way to get a lot of money and distance themselves from his father's choke hold. Clyde had always felt like the charity case at work and had vented his frustrations to her numerous times. But the money and bonuses had been great, and the structure the job afforded Clyde brought some semblance of normalcy to his abnormal lifestyle. Until the weekend.

Weekends were crazy. Friday nights included a good dinner prepared by Clyde, with a bottle of wine for Joanne and vodka or rum for him to wash down a couple of Percocet. An Ambien at bedtime used to do the trick, but its effect weakened as their drug abuse deepened. Saturdays began at noon with Bloody Marys to dull the edge from the previous night, usually followed by Pete dropping by to get stoned, have some drinks, and tinker on the various projects Clyde had going. Saturday night was like Friday, and Sunday mirrored Saturday. Monday rolled around too early for either of them, but a Xanax got them to work and through the day. Their lives were abusive and crazy, but somehow structured. When he left his job, the weekend was everlasting for Clyde. Joanne saw a marked change in her husband as he searched unsuccessfully for another way to earn a living. Pete worked and she worked, so Clyde was home alone to cultivate his growing depression.

Seeing him crack last year with the accidental overdose should have been her wake-up call. His current depression had her second-guessing whether it really had been an accident, but she was too afraid to confront Clyde about it, for fear of another attempt. She had come home from work and found him unconscious on the floor. She thought he was dead, and that had scared the hell out of her. That night at the hospital, she knew she needed to change her life, but how? She readily admitted to herself that she was scared to change anything. That's why she drank. She drank to escape the harsh realities of life, to escape the tough choices of life, simply to escape life itself. Throughout that winter, with Clyde in the hospital battling to breathe on his own again, she came to realize that her marriage was going to end prematurely—either with Clyde dying or her leaving.

But she couldn't leave, wouldn't know where to go if she did. They needed each other, so she helped nurse him back to health, hoping he could somehow gain some semblance of control over his demons. He kept talking about the dragon that came for him at night when he was alone, after she had gone to bed. He always felt its presence or smelled its rancid breath before it appeared, and when it finally did, he was paralyzed with fear; he could only watch helplessly as the monster spewed its fire and enveloped him with a roar so ghastly it had him begging for death. Hell had truly entered his soul, and there was no escape.

"What's a normal life?" he asked her. "Have we ever been normal?"

He was right. They had never been normal. They were both on dates, occupying adjoining tables, when they met at a restaurant in the mid-nineties. They struck up a conversation and exchanged phone numbers, all while having dinner with their dates. How normal was that? But that's how they met, and their relationship flourished because of their mutual love of sex, drugs, and rock 'n' roll.

"Please, just promise me I won't have to beg you not to kill yourself. You'll be killing me, as well," she said mournfully.

The vodka that Clyde was drinking was having the desired effect. He was becoming calmer, she thought, so maybe he would be able to sleep tonight.

"Okay, I promise you I won't try this again anytime soon," he lied, hoping she wouldn't notice. Why would she? She was only looking out for herself, anyway. She didn't care if he tried again as long as she wasn't around, and he would make sure of that. He continued to lovingly stroke Bear, while Joanne finally seemed to be relaxing with her wine.

The room began to darken and the walls started closing in around him, triggering the claustrophobic response he had come to expect. His breathing became shallow and his heartbeat quickened. He tried to will the fire-breathing monster away, as he had tried to do so many times before. As he peered into his soul, closing his eyes and quieting his breath while praying for a reprieve, the monster pulled back, vanishing into the fast receding walls. His depression had passed, and he knew why: soon this would all be over.

Time to crash—maybe get a little sleep, maybe not. Clyde finished the vodka and slowly stood.

Joanne, lost in her wine mixed with a healthy dose of adrenaline, snapped out of her haze when Clyde stirred. She had been having another nightmare about what had almost happened. She would have to leave him if he continued with this insanity. She really didn't want or even deserve to find his head splashed red against the wall one night after work, but she knew she probably would if she stayed. She needed to leave, but again, she didn't know where to go.

Clyde bent down to kiss her, saying, "Why don't you go to bed. I've caused enough excitement for one night. I'm just going to stay up with Bear and have another drink."

"Are you sure you'll be okay?" she asked.

"Yeah, go to bed. I'll get the lights," he replied and leaned down to give her another kiss and help her up.

"Your Honey Bear will always love you, my valentine," she mumbled, returning the kiss.

As she walked to their bedroom, he moved to the bar and found the next vodka bottle, opened it and poured himself a stiff drink, not bothering with ice, and returned to the couch. He sat down, took a drink, and lit up a joint. As he inhaled the fragrant smoke, his thoughts returned to Dagger. That name was so appropriate now. He missed their friendship but could never forgive him. Dagger was the reason he was at this place, wanting to end his life. Everything had been going along just fine until that asshole grew a conscience and called his family.

Christ, what a prick! Clyde threw his drink into the fireplace. The shattering of glass snapped him from his cauldron of anger. He knew Joanne was passed out and hadn't heard it, so he got up and poured himself another vodka, laughing at his predicament. He returned to the couch and began reminiscing about the good times, when Dags was Dagger and a ton of fun. He remembered Las Vegas, 2:00 a.m., money gone, and them licking their wounds in a hotel room, bonding. As much as he believed he could handle any drug cocktail, what Dagger did had always impressed him. The guy could spend the day drinking, gambling, and snorting coke, and as the night deepened, he would add some weed to the mix. When he felt he absolutely needed to crash, he would snort some coke, smoke a joint, take a sleeping pill, and wash it all down with a beer. Then he would lie down and hope the sleeping pill did the job. It always did, and the next morning those dagger eyes always opened, ready to pierce the coming day. Dags was lucky to be alive twenty-five years later to bust Clyde to his father. *What the fuck was that all about?*

Clyde knew that when he obsessed about Dagger, his abusive tendencies got worse. He also knew there was no way to stop them. He refilled his glass and washed down a couple of Xanax. The sleeping pills hadn't been working—nothing had really been working lately—but he added a couple of Ambien to the mix anyway. Maybe he would just go for it tonight and see what happened. An old buddy of his had tried that and died. It wasn't a suicide, just an overdose that wasn't really accidental. Maybe an experiment that turned fatal. What did it matter? Dead was dead.

After he finished the joint, he poured another drink and lit up a cigarette, initiating the coughing fit he had grown used to. He remembered how much fun he and Dagger used to have trying to kill themselves years ago, when they were young and strong and nothing could stop them. A small laugh escaped him as he remembered a night at his parents' house—they were out of town, of course—when he and Dagger had stayed up till morning watching classic movies, playing backgammon, and shooting coke. Dagger didn't like needles, so he had been the injector. Clyde could still taste the cocaine breath as the drug hit his veins. What a rush, what a fucking blast as they challenged death and won! What happened to that fun? He began silently singing Lou Reed's "Heroin" as he transported himself back to a more innocent time:

> When I put a spike into my vein
> Then I tell you things aren't quite the same
> When I'm rushing on my run
> And I feel just like Jesus' son
> And I guess I just don't know
> And I guess that I just don't know … Heroin

What a memorable night that had been, cheating death and loving it. He stared into the abyss of the fireplace, realizing that he no longer felt that urge to cheat death.

He petted his ever-faithful Bear, who was sharing the couch with him. "How could he do this to me? Why?" His mumbles faded as the pills finally began to dull his senses. "Please let me sleep tonight, Lord, please," he said, as he extinguished his cigarette and lay down on the couch. "Please let me sleep, let me sleep."

Sleep mercifully came to him that night. The dragon stayed caged.

10

Sterling returned from the market with a beautiful piece of grouper and a half pound of fresh shrimp. Madeleine would be arriving soon, but she had plenty of time to get things ready. She let out a giggle as she began preparing the fish. This was exactly what her heroine was doing in her novel, except for one glaring exception: Sterling was readying for her daughter, not her lover. Tonight she was making fish tacos. She grated some cheese, sliced a ripe avocado, and prepared a mango salsa, mimicking the main character in her book. Mother and daughter both loved Ferrari-Carano chardonnay, so Sterling had chilled two bottles. Given her recent revelations, this promised to be a late night.

She was about to make a salad when she heard Madeleine arrive. She stopped in mid-prep and ran out the door. There she was, looking so much older than her twenty-three years. Their hug was longer and tighter than usual as they relished the uniqueness of their relationship.

Sterling pulled back. "Let's have a look at you," she said. "Honey, you're so precious to me. I have been so wrong to hide anything from you."

Madeleine's hair was blond like her mother's, but she had her father's piercing emerald eyes, angular features, and tall frame. She had become quite beautiful.

Sterling initiated a second hug, saying, "I am so very sorry, dear."

"Oh Mom, I told you not to worry about it. This will be an exciting adventure for us, except for the service, of course. That will be hard, but I get to spend some time with you and Aunt Beth. We can explore your old haunts."

"Maddie, I'm sure my old haunts are long gone, but maybe Beth can introduce us to some new ones," Sterling said with a laugh. "Let's have a glass of wine and catch up until sunset."

Madeleine grabbed her bag from the car and followed her mother into the cottage.

Sterling opened a bottle, poured two glasses, and led the way out to the porch, where some chilled gulf shrimp cocktail awaited. Looking out on the courtyard, they nibbled on shrimp in a warming, comfortable silence for a few moments before Sterling asked Madeleine what she had been up to.

"I told you, Mom, I went to a really fun concert last night."

"Right. The Killers?" Sterling rolled her eyes in mock sarcasm.

"Mom, they're good. You would like them. They're edgy, with a great beat. But let's concentrate on tonight." She smiled and raised her glass to meet Sterling's. "Do you feel like talking about my father? Maybe fill me in so I don't throw something at him instinctively when I see him? That would sort of detract from your friend's service, don't you think?" Madeleine laughed and clinked her mom's glass again.

"Honey," Sterling said, smiling, "you have your father's features and his sharp sense of humor. That kept me going for a long time because I had so much of him in you." She paused briefly as she and Madeleine shared a look. "Then, as my writing began to take over and I was busy raising you, I stored his memory in a dark and quiet place, as one might with a close friend who had died. The years melted away, other relationships came and went, and it became easier not to explore that chapter with you." Sterling moved closer to Madeleine, gently grabbing her hand. "But we were very close, Clyde, Dags, and I. Oh, your father's name is Dags Bissell, and I have neither seen nor heard from him since before you were born. Clyde was his best friend. This is going to be very hard." She took another sip and gazed toward the gulf. "As I was saying, I dated Clyde briefly when I was young, and Dags was his best friend. They did everything together—many fun things, some not-so-good things too. Dags was very secretive about how he made money and would noticeably pull away whenever I broached the subject. I knew they were into drugs, like many of us were back then, but it might have gone a little deeper than that with him."

"Was he a drug dealer?"

Sterling withdrew her hand and turned to refill her half-full glass. "I'm pretty sure he was. But again, I didn't ask much. In hindsight maybe I was afraid of his answer. I know they took a lot of trips together, either fishing in Florida or gambling in Las Vegas. They loved hanging out with their pals. Anyway, I found him irresistible in spite of that, so after Clyde and I broke up, we began seeing each other. Maddie, I was so in love with him, but I was young. I remember that he started getting a little distant, which he tended to do occasionally, but this time I was more worried. I didn't want to lose him and had begun feeling like I could spend the rest of my life with him, which back then was a rarity among our group of friends. We were all single and carefree. Then one day he was gone."

"Gone? Just like that, gone?"

"Pretty much, dear. Clyde told me that he'd gone out West, probably to Las Vegas, and that he didn't know when he was returning. I knew Clyde knew and was being purposefully vague, and I realized I needed to pull back from him as well. Then I discovered I was pregnant. You pretty much know the rest."

It was closing in on six o'clock, so Sterling suggested they take a small cooler with the wine and shrimp and head to the beach in the golf cart. The sunset held a special place for them. For years they would take a spring vacation and fly to the Caribbean—usually Tortola, but sometimes Saint Thomas or Saint John. Many evenings they would walk to the beach and watch the sun set on what had been a glorious day of snorkeling, sailing, or simply marveling at the mysterious, beautiful sea. Sunset was their special time together.

They drove the four blocks to the beach, parked the cart, and renewed their cocktail conversation.

"How is your writing coming?" Madeleine asked. "Any exciting new heroes you can share with me?"

"I haven't been able to write a word since Clyde's death. I heard some awful story that's floating around Wilmington, some details about his death from Beth. Apparently Dags had recently moved back to Delaware and was concerned about Clyde's health. I don't know if an intervention ever materialized, but they had a falling out. Beth heard that Clyde's final words before shooting himself were a malicious phone call to Dags."

"Was Dags still on the phone when he shot himself?" Madeleine asked, shuddering at the thought.

"I don't know, dear," Sterling replied. "Pretty gruesome stuff, though. I never thought the two of them could ever reach such a violent place."

They drank in silence, each lost thought. A sudden breeze off the gulf brought them back.

"It is so beautiful and peaceful here, Mom," Madeleine remarked. "You did the right thing by moving here. It's safe, the people are nice, and it's a great place to raise a family. You don't have to worry about angry friends with guns." She shuddered again. "He must have been really sick to do that."

"Yes, Maddie, he must have been. To say what he said, and then do what he did, he must have been profoundly ill." She paused, looked at her daughter, and then said in a quiet voice, "Thanks again for coming, dear. This trip will be so much better with you."

"Have you ever seen the green spark at sunset?" Maddie asked, changing the subject.

"Now that depends on how much I've had to drink," Sterling said with a laugh, "and what kind of dream I'm dreaming. Maybe we'll see it tonight."

They didn't but imagined they may have before returning to the cottage for dinner. Sterling's cottage was a simple two bed, two bath in the historic district of Boca Grande—this designation simply making it harder to renovate. So the women were content to enjoy the beauty of the home's overly expansive courtyard.

Sterling poured two more glasses of wine and brought them out to Madeleine, who was watching two cardinals begin their dance of spring on a broad palm leaf. Sterling sat down and joined the audience. After a moment, the female flew off with the male in hot pursuit. Sterling faced her daughter, not knowing where to begin.

Madeleine made it easy. "You never wanted to find the man you loved?"

"No," Sterling replied firmly. "When he left, I made some difficult choices. I needed to take care of you, which meant taking care of myself. Maddie, he walked out on me. He didn't love me anymore, so my decisions in life were never based with him in mind. I was hurt and angry for a long, long time. He was a smart guy. If he had wanted to find me, he could have. But he didn't, and I couldn't afford to get distracted from raising you." She grabbed Maddie's hand and looked away, made uncomfortable by the memory of this sad time in her private life.

Another soft evening breeze temporarily interrupted their conversation. The cardinals returned and resumed their ritualistic singing, allowing Sterling to tamp down the emotions stirred up by her daughter's inquisitiveness. She lightened the mood with a complimentary remark about the end result being her jewel of a daughter, and then got up to finish making the salad and preparing the grouper.

Madeleine followed her mother into the kitchen and began slicing some tomatoes and a cucumber.

"Do you ever think about him?" she inquired, letting her mother know she wasn't backing off from learning as much as she could about the man who was her father.

"Every time I look at you," Sterling replied with a smile. "You have his face and his personality. He has always been here with us; I just didn't let you know that. I got over my emotions and simply treated him like your late father."

Madeleine moved closer to her mother and took her hand. "Mom, I never really shared this with you, but I did occasionally miss having a father. I would never change what we have and the love I have with you, but there were moments when I wondered what it would be like to have a loving father. You were such a perfect mother that I felt greedy wondering what other children experienced, having two nurturing parents. But then I saw the fractured families of my friends and classmates, and I felt lucky to have you." Madeleine sipped her wine, feeling her anticipation of meeting this man begin to grow.

Sterling went back outside, lit the grill and the tiki lanterns, and set the courtyard picnic table for dinner. The cardinals bade good night with a series of *wheets* and flew away. Nothing Madeleine said had surprised Sterling, who usually welcomed such exchanges, but this discussion was new—not necessarily uncomfortable, but something Sterling should have been better prepared for.

Madeleine brought out the grouper on a platter, and Sterling laid it gently on the grill, having rubbed olive oil on the grate as well as on top of the fish. She sat with Madeleine at the table. The tiki lanterns cast a warm glow over the two women, the flames mesmerizing any neighboring creatures that cared to watch.

Sterling struggled to find the right words before beginning. "Honey, you're just starting out in your life as a young adult. You have many friendships on different levels, but right now they're relatively new. Many of your current friends will disappear as they move, marry, and start families. Sadly, some will die young."

Madeleine gently interrupted. "What are you trying to tell me, Mom? So far, you're saying the obvious. I'm grown now. So what's up?"

"You're not grown, Madeleine," Sterling replied, beginning to smile, "but you're close. Really, really close. What's up is what we will be confronting in Delaware in the next few days. Where do I begin? Assuming Dags Bissell is there, I will be confronting twenty-four years of complicated feelings that I thought I had buried long ago. You may be meeting your father for the first time. How will you react? Christ, how will I react?" Sterling stood up and went to the grill to check the fish. "How is Dags dealing with losing a once-dear friend who punctuated his exit with such insane hatred?" She began absentmindedly brushing more olive oil over the fish. "Honey, the richness of our lives is usually defined by our relationships. At the end of the day, how do we look back on our lives? My relationship with Dags failed, but will this trip give us the opportunity to renew it on a different level that could lead to a new beginning for us all? In a full life, many relationships fail, a few survive, and even fewer thrive. When we lose a relationship that once thrived, like mine with Dags, and certainly Dags's with Clyde, we have lost an irreplaceable treasure." She did a quick check on the fish. "To be continued," she said. "Let's eat."

Madeleine loved her mother's fish tacos, and grouper was her favorite fish. She was instructed to sit while Sterling prepared her taco: first sprinkling a soft tortilla with grated mozzarella and cheddar cheese and microwaving it for thirty seconds; then adding the grouper, which she'd cut into small pieces, and topping it with mango salsa, some sliced avocado, a spoonful of sour cream, and finally—Sterling's pièce de résistance—a smidgeon of very finely diced bacon sprinkled over the sour cream. A side of black beans and a glass of white wine, and they were good to go. The wine was affecting them, but Sterling wanted to finish her thought.

"We were discussing relationships, weren't we?" she asked.

Madeleine let out a laugh, defusing the seriousness of her mother's question. "Mom, we weren't discussing; you were lecturing. But I loved what you were saying, so please continue." Another laugh escaped her.

Sterling smiled, trying to regain her composure and recapture a moment that had long ago vanished. She knew it was fruitless to pursue her "relationship" discussion (or lecture) with Madeleine. A mother has only so much serious time with a twenty-three-year-old who has everything in front of her. But before she threw in the towel, she added, "As you grow, you will learn to define relationships— what makes them thrive and what destroys them. When you think you have figured it all out, something like this will happen, making you shake your head at the sheer randomness in our lives. Now, that is another intellectual topic we will need to discuss at a later date." She reached over to give her daughter a hug. "You have always unknowingly kept the three of us connected. For your sake more than mine, I hope you get to meet him." She shot Madeleine a grin before adding, "Oh hell, if he's there and we chicken out, we can always stalk him."

11

An early taste of spring greeted us on the day of Clyde's service. The morning air was still and crisp, awakening the nostrils with each breath. The sun sparkled off the melting snow, giving the sky an unnatural hue of blue. The winter had been uncommonly harsh for the mid-Atlantic states, with blizzards and cold snaps that were more appropriate for Vermont than Delaware. Funerals and memorial services are always better begun with a beautiful day for celebration rather than a somber, gray day of mourning, so this day held promise.

I had spoken with my brother, Jack, regularly since the shooting, and he had persistently insisted that I attend. I'd kept my intentions from him until this morning, when I agreed to attend but said I would be arriving late and leaving early. In spite of my animosity toward Joanne, I was sensitive to her grief and didn't want to add any drama to a traumatic day. Katy, true to her word, wouldn't be joining me. I was okay with that, simply from the standpoint of not wanting her to make a scene if she saw Joanne. I wanted to control my secrecy as much as possible, so flying solo seemed like the prudent way to go.

The service was being conducted at Christ Church in downtown Philadelphia. I could have taken the train and walked the few blocks to the church but decided to drive so I could enjoy the weather and adjust my attitude. I was having a hard time. My theory about Clyde's final good-bye was being severely tested; I wasn't yet buying into it. His last words to me were still too close, still too raw for me to fully understand. I believed attending this service would become the first step in the healing I so desperately needed.

I had spent the previous nights staying up late and drowning my sorrows without Katy knowing. I wasn't eating because I wasn't hungry, and I spent each day either in a fog or talking with friends who tried futilely to cheer me up. Liquor, wine, and beer had been my sole companions, and I was getting along famously with all three.

This morning I had awakened thinking, *Fuck this self-pity,* and with that my outlook began to improve. After a long, hot shower involving multiple pep talks to myself, I emerged with a stronger attitude based not on self-pity but on anger about what Clyde had said to me. *What a coward! Plan a surprise attack, then flee? Fuck you! Katy was right. What a fucking asshole!* Decades ago I had counseled Clyde on relationships by saying the best way to heal from a broken one is to turn that lost love into hate—you get over it fast. You may not heal, but you get over it. That's what I was doing now, at fifty years old. I was remembering an immature, sarcastic twenty-something's advice and following it. But you know what? It was working. I needed to get past my self-pity, and this was the easiest short-term method to use. Later I could explore the more complicated route.

I decided to take Route 52 from Wilmington to Route 1 and drive through some of the Brandywine River Valley. Its rolling hills are steeped in history—from the Battle of the Brandywine in 1777, when the British general Sir William Howe outmaneuvered George Washington to capture Philadelphia, to the immigration of the Du Pont family in 1800 and the creation of their mansions, gardens, and museums. Many innovations sprouted from the early settlers to the valley. The log cabin and Conestoga wagon were introduced by the immigrant Swedes and Finns in the early 1600s. William Penn brought religious tolerance to the area in the form of his Society of Friends, better known as Quakers. Milling operations flourished along the river, and the Brandywine became the leader in the export of meal, flour, paper, and eventually gunpowder.

In the late 1960s, a group of concerned citizens captained by the Brandywine Conservancy set out to conserve thirty-two thousand acres of land in order to preserve its history, often through the philanthropic efforts of the Du Pont family. The Brandywine River Museum, located in the heart of the valley, evolved to house three generations of Wyeth paintings and illustrations.

I grew up in the valley but left in my twenties, feeling the need to get lost in the culture of the Wild West, and I'd only recently returned, so I was reacquainting myself with a rich history that I had ignored in my youth. I did remember taking a school field trip to Brandywine Battlefield State Park, where our class was divided into two sides, the British against the colonists. We loaded flour into socks, tied them off, and had a mock battle of sock flinging. If you got hit, a patch of flour was visible on your clothes, marking you as "killed" and no longer able to play the game. It was similar to dodge ball and an ingenious way to get kids to relate to history. This game must have been an innocent precursor to the paint gun wars of today.

During the American Revolution, Route 1 was known simply as the Great Road, so it seemed only natural for me to take that road to Philadelphia, our nation's first capital, to a pre-Revolutionary church. I was dressed in my navy-blue suit, a pink shirt, and a blue silk Jim Thompson tie I had discovered in my father's closet after he died. Katy had checked me over, straightening the tie and brushing lint off my jacket in her naturally maternal way, before giving me a soft kiss, lightly rubbing my cheeks, and reminding me not to make a scene (now saying it with a smile on her face). I returned her kiss and told her I loved her and didn't know what time I would be home. I went out to my car, took in a deep breath through my nose, and actually rejoiced at the magnificence of the day. Then I put Mark Knopfler's *Sailing to Philadelphia* in the CD player and began the drive to my late friend's funeral. Certainly in no hurry, I took in the scenery more than I normally would, enjoying the barn ruins, the occasional seventeenth-century house, and the small towns that lined my route.

The traffic began to increase as I neared the city, but as it was Saturday, I wasn't too concerned. My GPS led me right to the church. What a beautiful structure. The day was so bright that the sun seemed to glisten off the bricks, bathing the steeple in a brilliant white. As a distraction during my late nights since Clyde's death, I had googled the church to learn a little about its history. The first structure was built in 1695, but the one at which I was now marveling was begun in the 1720s and completed in 1744, with its impressive steeple added in 1754. At the time, the church was the tallest building in North America at two hundred feet. It was known as "the nation's church" because of the number of Revolutionary War heroes who had worshipped there, including both George Washington and John Adams when they were president. A few blocks away was a historic burial ground where Ben Franklin and four other signees of the Declaration of Independence were buried. The church began as Church of England, but after the war it evolved into an Episcopal church, and it had remained that way.

I was lucky to find a parking spot nearby. When I texted Jack to see where he was, he replied that he was about to go inside, where the family was already seated. Translation: it was safe to leave my car.

I walked to the entrance, following some people I vaguely knew, nodded to a couple of old friends, and entered the church. I was still wearing my sunglasses so I could privately scan the interior and select a spot. The stairs were to the left, and some mourners were already climbing them, so I followed. The balcony was not yet crowded. I took a seat in the front pew to better survey the congregation—that is, my friends and enemies.

The church was rectangular, with two rows of pews running lengthwise, seating four people in each pew; its narrowness added to its charm. Behind those rows, running below and underneath the balcony, lay more typical pews stretching wall to wall. The pulpit seemed to tower above the congregation, creating the intentional illusion that the preacher was closer to God than the rest of us. Yet we in the balcony were closer still.

My analysis was interrupted when someone sat down next to me. I glanced at the two women, whispered hello, and then returned to my spying. Something wasn't quite right. Wait—I recognized the older woman. It was Sterling Rodgers, my old girlfriend. I rested my head in my hands, almost like I was praying, and quietly uttered, "Shit." What to do? Did she recognize me? I looked over at them again, but they were whispering to each other; I couldn't confirm that it was her. But as soon as they stopped and returned their gazes to the front, I knew. I hadn't even considered that she would be here. I was so wrapped up in the shock of everything that I had been through that I'd neglected to think who else might attend.

When I moved to Wyoming, I'd fled from her in an immature, cowardly way. I wasn't going to be a coward again. I nudged her. "Sterling?"

She looked at me and momentarily blanched. She recovered quickly, politely grabbed my hand, and whispered, "Dags Bissell. God, it's been a long time." Trying to regain her composure, she continued, "I would like you to meet my daughter, Madeleine." She turned and whispered something to the young woman, who glanced at me quickly and said, "Hi."

This is where the uncomfortable pause set in, so I whispered, "Can we catch up later?" She nodded and we both withdrew to our own thoughts. Something still didn't seem right, but I ignored the gnawing feeling and returned to gazing at the congregation below.

Never having been religious, I sang when instructed and prayed when beseeched, neither knowing nor caring what words were uttered. Clyde's brother then rose to give the first eulogy, a dispassionate speech delivered by rote. My initial reaction was to conclude that he didn't care about Clyde, that possibly he was even happy that Clyde was dead because now their father's company was his. He joked about their sibling rivalry, laughed about shared childhood events, and talked about young Clyde's girlfriends. He never showed sadness or even the slightest remorse. This speech—it was no eulogy—could have been read at Clyde's wedding. The man was disgusting; he had no soul. He was slick, and he was making me sick. I closed my eyes and took another deep breath to calm my bubbling anger toward him. I rested my head in my hands again and closed my eyes. Clyde never had a chance around these people.

They were all toxic, and so was I, for not realizing what had been happening over the past six months.

When Clyde's brother was done, he gave himself a self-satisfied smile and sat down, believing he had knocked us dead with his brilliance.

My brother then rose, slowly made his way to the lectern, opened his notes, and began. "My name is Jack Bissell, and I would like to thank all of you for attending this celebration of Clyde's life—a full yet challenging life cut short by his own choosing." Jack was never one to beat around the bush, and confronting Clyde's suicide at his funeral was a bold beginning. "To try and get through the shock and the sadness of these past few days, my family has concentrated on remembering Clyde's wonderful qualities—his big heart, his fierce loyalty, his generosity, and his laughter—never forgetting all the good times we enjoyed with him. For me and my family, and for so many of you, Clyde was much more than a dear friend. He was family. He never forgot a birthday or an important event. He was there for weddings, celebrations, graduations, holidays, and birthdays, especially St. Patrick's Day, his birthday that he shared with my wife, Lu. Since he didn't have any children, he took his many godfather duties seriously, and if a friend was having a baby, he would almost plead to be considered as a godfather. I believe he leaves eight godchildren to mourn his passing."

I was entranced by Jack's words, and so very proud of him for attempting to bring Clyde back to life.

"He particularly loved Christmas, a time when he could shower his godchildren with money, presents, and love. One Christmas Eve, he and Joanne came by for dinner, and after the kids had gone to bed, he assembled an aquarium for my oldest daughter. When he and Joanne returned the next afternoon for some present opening, he just couldn't contain himself. He asked Kristen if she liked Santa's aquarium, and when she gushed about how much she loved it, he said he had built it. From then on, Clyde was Clyde Claus to my three daughters."

I rubbed my eyes and gritted my teeth. Why had I not been there when Clyde was sick? Why wouldn't he confide in me? Was it because I was such an intolerant hard-ass? I had failed at my clumsy attempt to help him—failed miserably. My eyes welled as I returned my attention to my brother.

Jack paused, trying to collect his emotions. I knew that he hurt, that delivering this eulogy was especially hard for him because he never had any idea about Clyde's depression. His tears gave way to a smile as he continued. "I'm sorry. Clyde was a dear friend who has left us so suddenly. We're here to celebrate his life, not mourn his death. My brother, Dags, and he were close friends, and one of Dags's funnier stories was when he tried to explain Clyde's personality in a nutshell. He likened Clyde to an untrained golden retriever: he was constantly getting in trouble but showed such unconditional love that you couldn't stay angry at him long, and soon he would be creating such uproarious laughter that all would be forgiven.

"Clyde might be the only man ever to drive his Mercedes onto a golf course—yes, he knew the owner—with three golf bags in the open trunk, drive to the first hole, and tell the starter we were ready to play. The public was amused for about six holes; then some geese really angered him, so he began honking the horn." Jack glanced at the minister. "That's when something hit the fan." He paused and looked around at the congregation, reliving the story as he told it. "My point here is that we were all along for a wild ride whenever we were around him, and that ride is now gone.

"How will we remember him? Years from now, will we remember the act of three days ago, or will we be lying on a beach somewhere, gambling in a casino somewhere, or simply drinking with friends somewhere when a memorable moment passes in front of us and graces us with a smile? I know I will always miss his life and will strive not to mourn his death. We miss you, Clyde. You were a ray of sunshine in our lives. We will always remember you, and we will always love you. Our lives are less rich without you. Rest in peace, my dear friend."

Jack surveyed the congregation for a moment and then began to speak again.

"I'm not a religious guy, so what I say next is personal. When my father died, I was devastated, as many of you who have lost a parent have been. For years I cried whenever I had a dream about my father. Then one night, having gone too long between dreams, my father came to me. I was so happy to see him, and so sad when I awoke. I don't even remember the dream. All I remember was having the feeling that I had tasted heaven. I believe that Clyde's memory will bring each of us closer to heaven, and I look forward to that encounter."

As Jack folded his notes and returned to his seat, I was pinching the bridge of my nose and vainly trying to control my emotions. Jack had done it. He had captured Clyde perfectly in the moment, melding Clyde's actions into a loving tribute to a dear friend lost.

I felt a hand touch my elbow and looked over to see Sterling mouth, "I'm so sorry." I pretty much lost it there and began to weep quietly. She gently rubbed my back until the minister rose and ascended the pulpit to deliver his homily. This is where I emotionally withdrew. I had heard what I wanted to hear, and now was the time for private reflection. I pulled Sterling's hand from my back and held it as the minister began to speak; it felt so natural.

I tried to recreate Clyde's final moments on earth.

Our one life is so precious; I refuse to believe that people would destroy such a gift. What pushes people to kill themselves, an act that may be the bravest and certainly the hardest thing they will ever do? The older I grow, the more positive I seem to become: I love life. I desperately love life. So suicide to me is something I simply cannot understand. Sure, I know people feel backed into a dark and forlorn place without any escape possible, a place where every day is torture from the time they awaken until they go to sleep. And I believe young people commit suicide impulsively because their lives are often overwhelmed by pain and suffering. But mature adults have contemplated this final act many times before they finally accomplish it; they are well aware of the consequences. If they believe there is no way out, something in their brains must have shut down to allow them to move forward with this action. No right-minded man would leave a bloody, headless torso for his loving wife to find, yet Clyde did just that. People like that have reached a point where all they care about is removing themselves from this earth. Their souls have gone dark.

Clyde certainly didn't care that Joanne, who was afraid of life anyway, would find him and be further traumatized. That is how I rationalized his final words to me. Of course he hated me; he believed I took everything from him. But after Valentine's Day, after he failed to follow through with his suicide, his body, mind, and soul began to shut down in order for him to succeed the next time. So the Clyde I spoke with on the phone was truly demented. The words he spat at me did not come from the man I knew and once loved; they came from a cornered animal, and I needed to get over my selfish feelings of hurt and understand his final cry. The old Clyde dialed the phone to speak with me, but the sick and dying Clyde spoke those words. I guess that was my rationalization.

The minister was finishing up; it was time for me to leave. I might have felt better about my relationship with Clyde, but Joanne would soon be leaving, and I never wanted to see her again. I whispered to Sterling that I was going, and she said she would follow. As the final hymn's opening chords played, we quietly excused ourselves and descended the stairs, exiting into the sunshine.

"Would you like to take a walk?" I asked Sterling. Then, looking at her daughter, I said, "I knew your mom in a past life and would like to catch up a little, if you have time."

Madeleine looked at her mother and replied, "Would you mind if I walked with you to our car and waited there?"

"You're welcome to walk with us, Madeleine, but you might get bored with 'remember whens.'"

Madeleine nodded. "It was nice meeting you, Mr. Bissell, but I'll let you two catch up."

I extended my hand. "Call me Dags. You're a beautiful woman, Madeleine, just like your mother. I hope to see you again soon."

I looked over at Sterling. "Have you ever been to the cemetery? Ben Franklin is buried there. Would you like to walk over? I think it's only a couple of blocks."

"Sure," Sterling said.

Madeleine glanced at Sterling and said, "You know, I think I'll check out this church after everyone leaves. Call me when you're ready to go." She leaned in to give her mother a kiss and then gave me a quick wave.

Sterling and I walked in uncomfortable silence for a while before I searched for her hand. "Sterling," I said, struggling, "I don't know how to say this, but I am so very sorry for leaving you so long ago. At the time I thought I was leaving for a serious reason, but now I'm not so sure." Searching for words, I awkwardly continued. "Some decisions we make come back to haunt us sometimes, but when I saw you today, a long-ago feeling reawakened."

Sterling laughed. "Can I write that down? I'm a writer, and I could use a line like that in my current book." She squeezed my hand.

The ice was broken, and suddenly we were close friends again, without Clyde—which is probably how it always should have been.

"I'm a writer too. That's funny."

"What do you write?" she asked, flashing the smile I realized I had never forgotten.

"Certainly nothing important," I countered, enjoying the intimacy of the moment. "I began with the local paper, then I wrote some freelance articles, and finally I published a couple of books. I'm independently wealthy," I joked, laughing nervously at my stupid play on words as well as my failed attempt at sophisticated humor. "You have a beautiful daughter. Are you still married?" I had seen neither a ring nor a man.

Sterling was quiet for a while. "I had forgotten how you liked to pry. Wait, wrong sentence. I had forgotten how openly inquisitive you were," she said, letting an easy laugh escape. "So you want to know a bit about my past during your extended absence?" She looked at me, suddenly serious. "That's a long time, Dagger." She seemed to be lost in thought for a few moments. Then she said, "I'm a writer in Florida, on the Gulf Coast. I too have written nothing important, but I enjoy it and it's what I do."

We came to the cemetery and entered, changing the direction of the conversation. Glancing over, I saw an odd smile on her face.

"What are you thinking?"

Returning my gaze, she said, "This isn't the first cemetery you've brought me to. Remember the night at the Du Pont family cemetery?" Her smile broadened. "You're still a charmer, bringing me to another one."

"Cemeteries make me feel so alive—don't they you? And success breeds success," I replied, matching her smile.

The cemetery resembled an outdoor museum rather than a final resting place. It had a two-dollar admission fee and a brochure describing its history, with a list of some of the famous people buried there and a map highlighting those markers. The cemetery was so old that the etched writing on many of the more prominent markers had worn away and metal plaques with the original inscriptions had been attached to them. Many more inscriptions had disappeared entirely, forever taking the identity of the deceased with them. The burial ground (its proper designation) covered two acres and included hundreds of graves, with many markers having disappeared over time due to erosion. I opened the map, got my bearings, and began the walk to Ben Franklin's stone.

We resumed our conversation. "Are you married?" I pressed.

"No," she replied cryptically. "Are you?"

"I've been married for nineteen years to a woman I met soon after I moved to Wyoming. We never had any kids, which afforded us certain freedoms as our lives progressed. We moved back a year ago. Judging from Madeleine's age, you must have married shortly after I left." She was quiet for a moment. Sensing some agitation, I added, "I don't mean to pry, Sterling. I guess I'm simply hoping you have been happy, that's all. I'm asking for information and explanations I have no business asking about. Let's just keep walking and reacquainting ourselves." Hoping to lighten the mood by changing the subject, I said, "So, do you think anyone will be checking out our graves in a couple of hundred years?"

"Only if they like to swim," Sterling replied. "Madeleine has a directive to scatter me at sea."

Suddenly she stopped, grabbed my other hand, and looked me in the eyes. I drew her close and lightly kissed her lips. I knew it was wrong, but she didn't pull away. I kissed her again, this time a little harder, and our tongues met. Twenty-four years melted away, and I was again young, single, and in the arms of my lover. After a few moments she pulled away and hugged me, saying into my chest, "You still take my breath away. Your kisses were always so delicious." She drew in a breath and sighed. "Let's find a bench."

There was one nearby, so we sat down, still holding hands, with Sterling leaning against my shoulder. "I never married," she began, "because I never met Mr. Right. I was close once, with that relationship producing the true love of my life—my daughter, Madeleine."

"She is a beautiful girl, and so mature. How old is she?" I asked, instantly regretting another prying question.

Sterling sighed again and sat up. "This moment has been so magical for me, and I'm afraid what I have to say might ruin it. But I want to tell you something." She grabbed both my hands again and caressed them for a few moments before continuing. "Dags, Maddie is our baby girl—yours as well as mine. There, I said it."

I looked at her, confused, and was about to speak when she put a finger to my lips and stopped me.

"Let me finish, please. When you left so suddenly, I was devastated, and two weeks later I discovered I was pregnant. Clyde wouldn't tell me where you had gone and wouldn't say when or even if you were coming back. It didn't take long for me to realize you weren't coming back. I was pissed, I was hurt, and I was pregnant—a single pregnant woman in Wilmington, Delaware, of all places. If I had told Clyde that I was pregnant and you had returned, I never would have known whether you'd done it out of love or guilt. So I moved to Florida and started a new life. When my sister told me about Clyde's suicide, I realized I might see you here. I think I came simply because you might be here. It's funny that we ended up sitting next to each other. Anyway, I've said what I came to say. I'm not asking you for anything, and I am so sorry for keeping our situation from you. I had a responsibility to tell you a long time ago."

I pretty much heard nothing she said after "Maddie is our baby girl, yours as well as mine." I was a father and had unknowingly been one for twenty-three years? The complexity of my emotions was overwhelming. Thoughts of how I'd deserted Sterling, leaving her to be a single mom; the lost years of my own fatherhood; and the now-murky future awaiting me as a father and Katy as a stepmother combined to leave me speechless. But my immediate reaction was to think that I'd bidden farewell to an old friend today even as I welcomed two new ones into my life—that is if she, they, would have me.

My mind was racing, splitting in many directions: father, daughter, ex-lover, wife. Christ! How would Katy react to this news? Would she feel threatened or excited? I really didn't have a clue.

All I knew was that I now needed to hold Sterling again and tell her that I had always loved her. I cupped her chin in my hand and bent down to kiss her. I kissed one eye and then the other, I kissed her nose and I kissed each cheek as tenderly as I knew how before touching her lips. She responded and began kissing me in return, uttering a soft groan when she was finished. She pulled away and stated the obvious: "Dags, we need to stop this. This could so easily get out of control, and you're married." She breathed in some of the crisp air that was still lingering as the day tried to warm. "I'm pleased with your initial reaction, though," she added, and she burst out laughing. "Would you like to go meet your daughter?"

"Does she know?" I asked.

"Yes, I told her last night and we discussed it, which is why she is here with me. She wanted to give me some support in case you were an asshole." She grinned. "I believed in my heart that you would welcome this news and wouldn't run away again."

"Sterling, I never should have run away in the first place. I got into some trouble and felt that leaving town for a long while was the safe thing to do. Then I began a new life in Wyoming, got a job, fell in love, and changed some of my ways. My parents thought I was traveling for a year, but they did forward your letter to a mailbox I kept in Las Vegas. I never had the guts to answer you, and I knew you deserved an answer. So, as I'm prone to do, I pushed you away and moved forward, too afraid to look back. It's a self-defense mechanism I have used for years, at least until now. The last few days have been a complicated time that has me questioning many of my mechanisms, primarily in my relationship with Clyde, but now also with you and Madeleine." I grabbed Sterling's hand. "Let's go find her."

We left our bench hand in hand, and as we exited the cemetery, I took another look at a place that had quite suddenly formed a special bond in my heart. A burial ground signifying life's end had just created new life for me. The irony did not escape me.

We made the short walk to Sterling's car in silence. Madeleine was standing beside the car as we approached. She gave her mother one of those private looks I imagine every child has with a parent. Sterling smiled and squeezed my hand. Madeleine now knew. She walked up to me and calmly said, "You're an asshole for leaving my mother the way you did. If I wasn't so polite I might slap you, but my mother taught me better than that."

Taken aback by just about everything I had learned in the past hour, I was initially at a loss for words. Then I replied, "Not only do you have your mother's beautiful looks, but you also possess the same profane mouth." This wasn't what I'd wanted my first reaction to be to my newly found daughter.

Sterling jumped in, having imagined a more romantic moment. "Honey, what Dags did is for another time. Right now he wants to meet his daughter. Let's go someplace for coffee and get to know each other better." She turned to me. "Do you have some time?"

I nodded. "Since we're headed back to Wilmington, why don't we meet at a restaurant there?" Then I added with an abbreviated laugh, "Madeleine can ride with me." I both saw and felt the knives and quickly clarified. "I'm kidding, Madeleine. Look, I know this is a tense situation for you. Believe me, we all feel the same way. I didn't knowingly abandon you. Christ, your mom just laid this on me a half hour ago, so can we try to act civil, at least until we get to know each other?"

Sterling laughed again, saying, "Dags has a nonstop sense of humor that doesn't always work, dear. He is trying hard, so let's give him a shot."

Madeleine finally relented with a small grin of her own. Try as she might to play the hard-ass, I believed I was softening her attitude toward me. "Madeleine," I said, "would you mind following your mother and me to Wilmington? There is a little restaurant I know where we can have a nice lunch and do some catching up. It's also very public and the owner frowns upon violence, so I would feel safe from you two." I had them both smiling now. "My car is right around the corner."

On the way I texted Jack, complimenting him on his eulogy and saying I would call him later. No need to throw the "new uncle" story his way yet.

I figured we would return on I-95, which would be faster and easier than my earlier, meandering route. Sterling waited until I had negotiated the few turns and the I-95 entrance ramp before confronting me.

"Dags, before we talk about the present or the future, you are going to listen to a little about my past."

I jumped in. "Fair enough. But before you do, I want you to know how fortunate I feel reconnecting with you. You have always been with me; I just didn't know it. Oh, and you're more beautiful today than you were twenty-four years ago."

"Bullshit," she replied, giving me a long forgotten look that was gone as suddenly as it had appeared. "I was really hurt when you left. Forget about Madeleine for a moment. I loved you so much back then, and I thought you felt the same. To think I could be so wrong! My trust in human nature took a major hit from you. If I couldn't believe in you, if I couldn't trust you, then who could I believe in and who could I trust? I wanted to spend the rest of my life with you raising a family, and I didn't even get a good-bye." The hurt she was feeling was palpable.

"When I discovered I was pregnant, I was insistent on bringing our baby into this world with or without you. I wasn't getting another abortion. Remember, we did that once, and to be honest, I was never the same. I couldn't do it again, even though I really hated you. So I had to find the strength to continue on a positive path, primarily for Madeleine's welfare but ultimately for mine too. I've written fourteen books, and you are in some of them—just pieces of your character, or lack thereof, in some good guys and in some villains as well. So I guess I have kept a place for you too."

Sterling's phone rang, giving me a chance to breathe. It was Madeleine. Sterling listened for a moment and then said, "Sorry, dear. I think I'm making him feel uncomfortable." She took the phone from her ear and turned to me. "Slow down. You're making my daughter's life too dangerous."

"Our daughter," I mouthed, and Sterling returned to her call, promising I wouldn't set any more speed records.

I had nothing to say that would ease her anger, so when she hung up I replied, "I'm sorry. That's all I can say. I was the asshole you and Madeleine say I am. I like to think I've grown some since then, but after my relationship with Clyde, I'm having second thoughts."

Sterling softened and turned toward me, touching my hand. "What happened to you two? I heard an ugly story about what he said, but how did you guys reach that point?"

It was my turn to sigh and collect my thoughts. "Years ago, Katy threw me a birthday party at her parents' house in Vermont. All my siblings came, as well as some close friends, including Clyde and Joanne. From the outset they were both out of control, spilling red wine on the furniture, ignoring their mess, and continually falling down. Clyde hurt himself during one of the falls, and Katy had to do the bandaging because Joanne refused to. They were tedious to have around, but Clyde had always been so funny that we'd tolerated him. But he wasn't even funny this time. He was manic. The next day I heard he had been trying to pass out Percocet to everyone. He knew not to approach me with his offer. Oh, before the party he had bragged about this doctor who would trade one hundred pills for an ounce of top-shelf weed. He thought that was really cool, but when I didn't show a similar reaction, he knew I didn't approve. I got pissed with him for doing pills, and later I sent him an uncomplimentary photo of himself from the party with red wine spilled on his Brooks Brothers shirt. That pissed him off, and we didn't talk for a while. The following spring, I invited some friends down to Florida—we have a place on the East Coast—and Clyde was included. I pointedly told him to leave the pills at home, knowing he wouldn't, but thinking that at least he wouldn't eat so many. I think I'm rambling—and we need to take the next exit."

"I get the point," Sterling said. "But where is this going?"

"The point is I was alarmed about his health and worried that he might die soon. As much as I was growing tired of his pill-induced antics, he was an old friend and I didn't want to lose him. I don't make friends easily, and he was my most loyal friend. What Jack said in church about Clyde's loyalty was true."

Sterling interrupted again. "That's funny about men. Or not really funny—more odd really, even sad. Men don't make friends as easily as women. I wonder why?"

"I don't know, and I want to finish this before we reach the restaurant."

"Sorry. Please continue," she said, showing me I had her full attention.

"Anyway, the last time he came to visit, he looked really bad, even more manic than before, and he was eating a lot of pills. I had reached the point where I felt I needed to force him to get help. I cared about him and wanted to help him, and ultimately I made a clumsy attempt at intervention by going to his family. We believed the popular notion that the addict can only help himself and often needs to hit rock bottom before being successful in recovery. He didn't buy it and hated me from that point forward, and his rock bottom was firing a .22 bullet into his mouth. That's the story in a nutshell, and whatever you heard was probably correct. I was the last person he spoke to, and he left this world a very pissed-off man. Too bad; it could have been different if he had just reached out for some help."

Sterling had a pensive look on her face, and when I asked her what she was thinking about, she said, "I don't know, Dags. Some people can't be saved, and when we lose them, we shouldn't point fingers, especially back at ourselves. We are all so imperfect, so human. We make mistakes, we learn from them, and usually no one dies. Please don't be too hard on yourself. It wasn't your fault that Clyde died. I know it's fresh, but you're a good guy who tried his best. It sounds like Clyde was battling some serious issues."

"That's the weird thing about this, Sterling. I didn't try my best. I could have done so much more if I had truly cared about his welfare. But when he verbally attacked me to anyone who would listen, including my brother, I basically developed the same 'fuck you' attitude toward him that he had toward me. I wish I had known the depths to which he had fallen, but I didn't, and now he's dead. You know what you just said about men having a harder time making friends or forging close friendships? Clyde had hundreds of friends, and virtually none of us knew that he was suicidal. How is that possible?"

I took a right on Buck Road and a left into the Janssen's shopping center, where I easily found a parking place in front of Elizabeth's. Next up—Madeleine.

Elizabeth's is a high-end pizza restaurant in Greenville, a suburb of Wilmington and the gateway to the chateau country of the old Du Pont families. Everything there is expensive and top-shelf, including the pizza. A few outdoor tables greeted patrons, and inside, a beautifully ornate, brightly lit bar with two large flat-screen televisions beckoned the single guy. Beyond that was a welcoming dining room, and throughout the restaurant there were beautiful, black-and-white photos of many famous women named Elizabeth. That was the clue that hinted that the establishment wasn't named after its owner, but you never knew—maybe Elizabeth liked actresses with the same name. There was Elizabeth Montgomery, my favorite actress when I was a testosterone-filled teenager who found her entrancing in *Bewitched*. On a far wall was Elizabeth Taylor during her siren days, in *Cleopatra*. Queen Elizabeth II also graced these walls of fame.

I asked for a private table so as not to upset fellow diners should profane invective or silverware be tossed about. Our waitress took our drink orders. Madeleine ordered iced tea, and Sterling did too, until she heard me change my order from coffee to a Stella draft. She glanced at me with a barely perceptible grin and went with a Byron pinot noir; Madeleine changed to a house chardonnay. I was reminded of the scene from *Body Heat* when a roomful of lawyers and beneficiaries are arguing over the validity of a will, and everyone is tense until one lawyer asks if anyone minds if he smokes. Nobody does, and then everybody lights up except Ted Danson, who says he's happy inhaling the second-hand smoke from everyone else. In our real-life version, we were all ordering alcohol to relax. Certainly a promising start.

Our drinks came, and after testing the alcoholic waters, Madeleine began by apologizing for her behavior. "I know how embarrassed I made Mom at an incredibly sensitive time for both of you. It was a beautiful service, and the eulogy … was that your brother?" I nodded. "I could feel his heartfelt words. He really loved Clyde, as I'm sure you did. I'm really sorry for your loss."

"We both are, Dags," Sterling said. "We know how much he meant to you. Life is so precious, and the intentional taking of one's own life is especially tragic." She sipped her wine and began to study the menu.

"He was a good guy with insurmountable problems who could no longer function like we do," I replied. "Look, I don't want to sound cold, but let's order some lunch and talk about someone other than Clyde. Why don't you beautiful women catch me up on what I've been missing these past twenty-three years? But no prying, and if I do stray that way, remind me nicely. Let's toast to old and new friends." We clinked glasses, repeating the toast.

For lunch, the women ordered salads—Sterling going with a fruit, walnut, and bleu cheese salad that included pear and apple slices with a red onion and balsamic vinaigrette, while Madeleine ordered a Greenville Cobb, which consisted of chicken, red onion, bacon, tomato, and field greens with a light raspberry vinaigrette. I ordered a Shue pizza (named after Elizabeth Shue, another big-screen fantasy of mine), topped with barbequed chicken, mozzarella, and fontina, and garnished with scallions.

The meal lasted a couple of hours as I watched mother and daughter interact like best friends. And why wouldn't they be? It had always just been the two of them. I wondered where I would fit into the mix, if I were lucky enough to fit in at all. My mind drifted to Katy. I'd have to deal with this delicately with her. I was under no illusions that I would skate through this unscathed, without some sort of a confrontation. She would always be pissed at Clyde for his evil words but had softened this morning as I left. Now I had to return and somehow explain the events of this afternoon. Having already had a couple of beers, I knew I was in for an exceptionally long night. There was no way I could postpone the discussion until tomorrow. Then again, maybe there was, right?

"Dags? Hello?" Sterling's voice brought me from my reverie. "Are we boring you already?"

"Sorry … this has been an emotional day for me. I was thinking about how my wife will react to all this. What were you saying?"

"What's your wife's name?"

"Katy."

"How do you think Katy will react?"

"She'll be shocked, maybe a little hurt that we never had kids. I don't know." Time to change the subject. "When are you flying out?"

Madeleine answered. "I'm leaving tomorrow afternoon. Mom has an open ticket. Do you think your wife might want to meet me tomorrow morning? I'm a little apprehensive about doing that."

"Maybe not this trip," I replied. How was I going to figure this out? I still had strong feelings for Sterling, but could those feelings simply be a case of nostalgia? I knew I wanted to see her again, maybe take a walk in the country and escape the present, just the two of us in a part-time fantasy. My feisty, Stella-infested libido was taking over, and I had no desire to tamp it down.

"Can I drive you to the airport tomorrow—one last chance to talk before you go?" Was I being too obvious?

"Why don't we both take our daughter to the airport?" Sterling replied. The ride back will give us a chance to talk some more." *Bingo!* I silently cheered to that libido.

12

After we left Elizabeth's, I walked the women to their car. We decided that I would pick them up at Bethany's the next day at noon. I hugged my daughter for the first time; she was timid in her response. Sterling and I exchanged equally timid pecks on the cheek before leaving. I sat in my car for several moments, trying to decipher the day and figure out my next move. What would I tell Katy? Nothing? Why not? So I decided to postpone discussion of this newly opened chapter until tomorrow and concentrate on Clyde's service for the rest of the day. My dead friend would help me one last time by covering for my distraction, and Katy would be her usual sympathetic and nurturing self without any more surprises. Her surprise would come tomorrow, maybe. *There I go again with my procrastination.* How long could I possibly delay this news? Possibly longer than most, if I played my cards right.

Our house was five minutes from Greenville, so I arrived home before I wanted to. A March cool was settling in as the sun crept west. The once-promising day full of remembrance and renewal was becoming stale as I left the car and slowly walked to my front door. The air was still. I was so depressed. My life sucked.

My depression began to dissolve when I opened the door and saw Katy reading on our couch, her reading glasses tilted down, her slightly graying hair falling in such a way as to hide those passionately sexy blue eyes that had bidden me "Come hither" so many years before, or, if you don't like Shakespeare, "Get over here, big boy!"

Katy had the gift of calm—with her soft-blue eyes, she could relax anyone she encountered—but when I came over to give her a kiss, those eyes looked concerned.

"Hey babe," I said as I reached down to kiss her, "I missed you." I knew something was wrong. I knelt down and gently turned her face to meet mine. "Is something bothering you?" I pulled her gently to her feet and then I held her and rubbed her back while I buried my face in her hair. That familiar scent. My emotions surprised me. I held Katy tightly, greedily; I didn't want to let go.

"I don't know." She paused a moment before pushing me away, keeping her hands on my hips. "You got a phone call a little while ago. Clyde's doctor, Merlin Sanders, called. I didn't recognize the number so I didn't answer, but I listened to his message."

"What did he say?"

"He said he would like to get together sometime soon and discuss Clyde. Here, listen." She dialed the prompts and handed me the phone. I wasn't prepared for yet another surprise today, and the thought of hearing the voice of Clyde's drug dispenser was a *Remind me why I woke up this morning?* moment. The anticipation made my skin crawl; I was about to hear from a man I sincerely wanted to kill. But the voice I heard came from someone different. A sad, tired, yet formal voice began by saying, "Mr. Bissell, my name is Merlin Sanders, and I was Clyde Colson's primary care physician. I am so very sorry for your loss. I know you were friends because he always spoke so highly of you. I was his friend as well. If you could find the time to call me the first of the week, I would appreciate it. Thank you."

I jotted down his number, thinking I needed to impose a news blackout for the rest of the day, and returned my attention to Katy.

"Honey, I've had a really long and weird day. I want to tell you about the service, but let me shower first. Then let's go out to dinner."

Katy seemed to brighten up. "I'll make an apple and cheese plate for after your shower. Oh, and I bought some sushi, so you're saved from your kind offer for dinner. But I will bank it for later. Now go get cleaned up."

Could a guy be so lucky? I was going to take a long, hot, cleansing shower and figure out how to tell her about Madeleine tonight, not tomorrow. So much for procrastination.

Procrastination in the shower was an invaluable weapon against the impulsive behavior I so adored, so I figured I had a good half hour to relax and control my emotions. I believed Katy would be pissed at first and then—I hoped—would embrace Madeleine as her daughter. Katy's honest beauty unwittingly demanded that I tell her the truth tonight. Okay, maybe not the making out with my old girlfriend part, but the important stuff. The Madeleine stuff.

The hot water was beginning to calm me, preparing me to offer a compassionate explanation for my new status as father. Until now, I had never needed to figure out how to tell the twenty-two-year love of my life that I had a daughter from a previous relationship. I concentrated on the pressure of the water as it massaged my head and neck. Bending down, I grabbed my knees so the water could loosen my back. I began to daydream. In my dream, Madeleine was a baby and Katy was my wife and her mother; it was just the three of us and our black-and-silver rescue dog.

As quickly as I'd retreated from reality, I was pulled back by Katy's knock on the door and entrance into the bathroom.

"I brought you a beer for after your shower," she said cheerily. "I'll leave it here on the counter. Don't stay in too much longer or you will turn into a prune and your beer will get warm."

Okay, it was showtime, and I still had no idea how to proceed. So I decided to wing it, putting an extreme amount of faith in the love of my life.

Katy watched as Dags made his way to the bar—her husband, her man whom she loved more each day than the day before. Was she a sap to think this way? She didn't think so.

She had been bartending in Wyoming when he sauntered in so many years earlier, looking awkwardly full of himself and reminding her of so many other men who had walked through that door. Men— they all thought they were powerful beings who owned the world, but really they were nothing more than needy little boys most of the time. Dags had ordered a beer and begun a clumsy flirtation, saying he was new in town and needed a job and a place to live, exhibiting the neediness typical of the guys she'd met there. He ordered some food and another beer, in no obvious hurry to leave. He was easy to look at and was nice enough, with a good sense of humor, and so she began to pay him a little more attention than before. At closing time, he asked if she wanted to go for a walk, and though she knew where this was headed, she agreed. Their walk led to her house and into her bedroom. He never left.

Katy knew Dags was pouring her a glass of wine so they could share some time together over an informal sushi dinner and he could discuss his day at Clyde's service if he wanted. He looked so tired, so defeated.

"How was the service?" she asked. "You're still in one piece, so you must have behaved yourself." They exchanged warm, comfortable glances. Still, he seemed distracted. "Is everything okay?" She made him a plate of salmon and yellowtail sashimi, mixing the wasabi with the soy sauce before adding some ginger. They each had a couple of bites before he felt like answering.

"Yes and no," he finally replied, and then he retracted the statement with "I mean yes. I've had a remarkable day. The church is a beautiful, pre-Revolutionary structure with a burial ground that must date back three hundred years or so. I didn't interact with any of the family, hence the one piece you're now seeing." A short laugh escaped Katy. "They never saw me, because I came late and sat in the balcony. Jack gave the most moving, heartfelt eulogy I have ever heard. He brought Clyde to life with old, fun stories that made me feel like I loved the guy again, and he succeeded in helping me begin healing from Clyde's phone call."

Bringing the bottle to his mouth, Dags gulped some beer before tiredly exhaling and meeting his wife's concerned eyes.

"Katy, I realize now there's nothing I can do about that call. I've spent a lot of time thinking about this. He made it, I heard him say what he said, and then he killed himself, leaving me few choices of how to respond. I know I'm going to be okay from this. I didn't know that yesterday, but I'm pretty confident now." He paused to take another healthy gulp and a bite of white tuna. "I saw a lot of friends from my past and happened to be seated next to this woman who used to be good friends with Clyde and me before I moved to Wyoming. She was an old girlfriend of both of ours—at different times, of course," he added, smiling at this uncomfortable situation of having to explain himself to her.

Katy raised one eyebrow in feigned interest. "Does this old girlfriend have a name?"

He knew she was just busting his balls in fun, and she knew he knew that, so this was nothing more than the playacting and lighthearted bantering they had grown accustomed to over the years. He played along, sliding a sexy look her way and saying, after a moment of silence, "She does."

He abruptly grabbed another piece of salmon and then headed for the fridge, suddenly parched, returning to the sofa with another beer and a bottle of chardonnay for her.

"Shall I pour?" he asked rhetorically as he filled her glass. He reminded himself that this was not just playacting and bantering; a serious admission had to be made, with yet-to-be-determined consequences to follow. He paused, tamping down the foreplay while gathering his senses, and cleared his throat. He took Katy's hand in his.

She looked him in the eye and said, "This is the *no* part, isn't it?"

Dags sighed, nodded his head, and answered, "Yeah." He moved closer to her. "Katy, I've loved you since the day I laid eyes on you back at the Silver Saloon. I love you more now than ever before, and I know in my heart that I will love you for the rest of our lives."

Katy didn't like where this was going. Whenever Dags talked like this, he had fucked up and was trying to apologize and make things right. But she let him continue uninterrupted.

"I know we chose not to have kids, and I realize that was a sacrifice on your part to accommodate me."

He wasn't thinking of adopting kids, was he? She was really getting nervous now.

He paused, careful with the nuance of his next sentence. "Honey, after the service, this woman, her name is Sterling Rodgers, told me that I had fathered her child before I moved to Wyoming twenty-four years ago. I had no idea she was pregnant when I left Delaware, and I left quite suddenly, without saying good-bye to her, like the immature guy I used to be. Her daughter was there, and I met her. Her name is Madeleine."

Katy froze. She was confident in their relationship but still had to ask, "So you have a daughter? What do you want to do? Do you want this Sterling Rodgers to be a part of our lives now?"

Dags was quick to respond. "Only as the mother of our daughter, and I want the *our* to be you and me."

He moved closer, taking her hands in his. "This is our opportunity to be parents, Katy. We were always too young, too occupied with our own lives, I guess always too nervous to have children and raise a family. Please try to accept this and welcome her into our family—not right away, of course, but ultimately. I want that more than anything, for us to help be her parents if she accepts me as an acting father. But the jury is still out on that."

"When do I meet her?" Katy asked. She was still numb. *I ask about a funeral service, and the answer is that I have a stepdaughter I didn't know about.* "Honey, this is too complicated for me to think about tonight. What are you going to do?"

"Madeleine is leaving tomorrow, but her mother is staying with her sister for a couple of days. I've offered to drive them to the airport, where I hope to form a clearer picture of where we all stand in this. I really want this to work for us—for all of us."

Katy stood up and went over to offer him a good-night kiss. "Then we will make it work. Together, the both of us. But let's begin tomorrow. I'm exhausted and confused, and you're overwhelmed. I'm going upstairs to read. You come to bed when you want."

She sure knew how to encapsulate things.

I felt lost, so I followed her upstairs. I was thankful that the night was finally over, the curtain drawing shut on another complicated day in my life. I sat on the bed and gave Katy a kiss good night, a kiss that was slow and tender. Then I gave her another kiss and a hug. "We'll work this out. Whatever you want is what we'll do. You're the most important person in my life. You know that."

"I know. I love you too," she whispered, opening her book. "Don't stay up too late. You've had a long day."

I went downstairs and picked at the remains of dinner before putting on a jacket and going outside. The air was still and cold, the warmth of the day long forgotten with the setting sun. The moonless night showcased the stars en masse as I stared into the infinity of space. I remembered being a boy and standing outside my house on a similar night, eagerly waiting for my father to return home from a business trip—thinking, hoping, that each moving light in the sky was his plane, that he would be home soon. I could never sleep until he came into my room to give me a hug and say good night. I was so happy to have him home.

Until now, my daughter had never had the chance to dream of her father's return. Perhaps tonight, she too was gazing at the stars, thankful that her father had returned from his extended journey. Could the magic I'd felt as a child permeate an adult heart? God, I hoped so. I buried my face in my hands and stifled a cry as I remembered my father and imagined all I had missed by not being a father—a chapter long closed, never to be read. After a few moments, I returned my gaze to the sky, silently thanking the gods for these memories, and then I went inside, praying that the past could infuse some hope into the future.

My night was restless; I slept fitfully as images from the day invaded my dreams. My dead friend visited me, appearing from nowhere to say that he was in a good place, peaceful at last. He said he loved me, said there was nothing I could have done to save him, said he would have chosen this path with or without me. That was his destiny, he said, and I was powerless to change it. Then he turned and walked into the fog, the smoke from his cigarette blending with the vapor. I yelled to him as he disappeared, trying to tell him that I forgave him for his words and that I should have been there to help him, but my voice was mute and he never heard me. I awoke with tears in my eyes, disoriented from reentry into reality. I looked at the clock: it was 3:00 a.m., the darkest hour of the night. I gritted my teeth to stifle the wave of sorrow that enveloped me. Could I ever get back to sleep?

I did. Another dream unfolded. I was a young man, and the little boy who stared at the stars was now my son. He came to me as I knelt down and offered me a little hug, burying his young, innocent face in my shoulder—his arms barely long enough to encircle my neck, his skin incredibly soft, his love for me so pure. It was just like heaven until something distracted me, and when I returned, my son was sitting with my father in a high-backed chair … but now I was the son as a five-year-old child, and my father had the face of his father holding his great-grandson. Four generations blended into one scene—three real and one imagined, forever lost, but all inexplicably connected.

13

The chaos of my dreams awakened me at dawn on Sunday. As my unconsciousness gave way to reality, I wrestled to recapture my sleep. My old friend, the man I thought hated me, had returned to apologize for his verbal attack. I had accepted his apology, and we had receded as friends. Or did I just make that up to conceal another truth? My imaginary son and my very real father and grandfather had blessed me with their presence. *Please don't take me away from this,* I prayed. *Let me float in this semiconscious cloud for just a little longer. I may never see them again.* I drifted off trying to recapture the magic of the past and fell into a deep, dreamless sleep.

When I awoke, I rolled over to find Katy gone. I looked at the clock. It was 8:30, way too late. What happened? Where was Katy?

Those dreams were so real … yet they were just dreams. Did the dead really possess the ability to visit our subconscious and make things right, to settle down the living by answering unanswerable questions? I wanted to believe that, but the reality was probably that they were simply dead, and my bruised brain was wrapping me in a protective cocoon.

As I looked out the window, I saw that the promise of yesterday was gone. In its place was a gray, monochromatic landscape: clouds shrouded the trees and a mist hung in the dense air, a slight breeze unable to dislodge the forbidding presence of gloom. Today I was facing an uncertain future as I acquainted myself with my daughter. The magic of the burial grounds would be gone as I began a task with which I was completely unfamiliar—that of pretending to be a parent.

Another shower was in order to relax me and erase the cobwebs and the memories of my sleep.

Katy was reading in the sunroom when I walked into the kitchen. She glanced up and smiled. "I was beginning to wonder if you were ever going to get up."

"I had a very unsettled sleep last night, and finally this morning, when I thought I would never sleep, I fell into the deepest sleep I could ever imagine. I guess yesterday really wore me out." Stifling a yawn, I poured myself a cup of coffee and sat down next to her, kissing her good morning. "Clyde came to me in a dream last night and said he was okay, that it wasn't my fault and that he had always loved me. Pretty weird, I guess, but I bought it."

Touching my hand, she replied, "What a beautiful experience, to have a friendship blossom after the friend has died."

I detected the light sarcasm; I knew that she was not about to forget the hurt Clyde had caused me when he called, but she was lending a sympathetic ear nonetheless.

"Then I had a discombobulated dream about being a father—this time to a little boy—and my father and his father were with me and my son. It was both confusing and moving. I woke up with so many conflicting feelings, primarily love and loss."

Katy rose from her chair and went to the kitchen. "Let me make you some breakfast," she said, grabbing a plate and a saucepan. "Maybe some poached eggs with an English muffin and that fresh OJ from Janssen's that you like so much?"

I could tell she was preoccupied, maybe even a little pissed. She turned to face me. *God I love it when I'm right … I think.*

"Dagger, we need to talk about this relationship of yours, and this daughter that may or may not want to be part of your life or our life together. That's all I've thought about all morning. For instance, are you absolutely sure that you're the father?"

Whenever she called me Dagger, she was being serious and softening me up for the kill. Katy serious was always something I tried to avoid.

"I'm really not that hungry." Better to die on an empty stomach. Saved on cleanup. "Let me toast a bagel and have another cup of coffee, and then we can talk," I said, trying to figure out my own agenda so I could clearly express it to her. I somehow knew I was the father, but I had to convince Katy of that and so much more.

What was my agenda with Sterling and Madeleine, and how could I make it work with without upsetting Katy?

I really needed to compartmentalize these three women. Katy was my wife. She was real; she was yesterday, today, and tomorrow. Her words and her feelings meant everything to me. And she could kill me.

Sterling was my first real love, a trusting young woman when I unceremoniously ditched her so many years ago. The feelings that I felt for her yesterday—the kissing, the caressing, the intimacy—were they real or just nostalgia?

Madeleine was our daughter—news that was thrust upon me at a sensitive time in my life. Why had Sterling told me about this now? Why hadn't she told me about it years ago? And was I simply feeling obligated to step up to the plate, or was fatherhood something I had missed subconsciously and now wanted in order to enrich my remaining years? Madeleine was the easy part of this female equation. My dreams answered the last question; I most certainly wanted to be an active father, if she would allow me to. But accepting and including Madeleine in my life meant including Sterling too, at least peripherally, and therein lay the rub. Could I keep my hands to myself? Hmmm. Did that "yesterday, today, and tomorrow" phrase also apply to Sterling?

With my breakfast done, Katy and I sat down for our talk. I was still thinking about compartmentalization and where that might lead. Katy jumped right in, obviously having stewed over the situation since last night.

"Dagger, have you thought about what you want to do and how this may affect our marriage?"

She didn't waste any time in delivering her salvo; I was already backing against the ropes, wondering what hit me. I didn't think "Whatever you want, dear" was appropriate here, but I tried it anyway, massaging the sentence with some subtle camouflage.

"I've thought about this, Katy, and whatever happens, I don't want our marriage adversely affected. I don't want to do anything to hurt you or us. Yesterday I went to a friend's funeral. That was all I had planned. Today I'm a father. I didn't ask for this, but it's here. It's reality now. I need to address it with you and, later, with Sterling and Madeleine. How you respond will affect my response to them. If you want me to walk away from this, I will." I wondered if the massaging had worked. I found out soon enough.

"This is really not the time for 'I'll do whatever you want.' You need to figure out what will work for the four of us. You can't just walk away from them because you think it will make my life easier, and I assure you it would, but that's beside the point. You are a father now, and that carries a responsibility with it. So again, have you thought about how you're going to handle this?"

As usual she cut to the chase, no bullshit. Why even try to skate around Katy's questions? I tried again, careful to avoid another onslaught. "If she will accept me as a father, and if she will accept you as my wife, then I would like to give this a shot." I stopped there to see if Katy was amenable to that answer.

Apparently she was, as she moved on to the next topic. "I know that this sounds cold-hearted, Dags, but how do you know you're the father?"

"Honestly, Katy, it never crossed my mind that I wasn't. The time line matches, and Sterling is successful in her own right. What of ours would she want? From what I've gathered, she and Madeleine have enjoyed a happy life. I just don't see her lying about this. And I saw a resemblance in both looks and personality. It was weird."

"What does Sterling do?"

"She's an author; I think she writes romantic novels. She lives in Boca Grande, Florida, where only the wealthy survive. I know actions speak louder than words, and I'll find out more later, but I believe she felt it was time, and the moment presented itself for her to open up about Madeleine. Christ, I was sitting next to them in church! That begged for the moment."

I could see Katy weighing these answers positively before moving on to her next query. I felt like I was being interviewed and would be summarily dismissed if she smelled any more bullshit. I had been duly warned.

"What kind of relationship do you see yourself having with Sterling?" Katy asked, and I quietly cringed. I'd seen it coming.

"I don't know yet. In a perfect world—"

"Dagger, this is not a perfect world."

"Look Katy, this is hard enough without your insensitive interruptions." My god, I stood up for myself. Score a point for me.

"That was not an insensitive interruption," she retorted, glaring right through me. "This is not a perfect world, so I don't need a 'perfect world' answer."

I immediately began backpedaling, deducting that point while trying to escape her attack. "I'm sorry for my theoretical answer; I didn't know I was on trial here. My intent is to be friendly with Sterling because we have a child together. I don't want to disrupt the life that we share here, and I don't want to include her in our life. Does that make any sense to you?"

I saw her begin to soften. "I'm sorry, Dags, I just feel threatened with this news. I keep thinking that our not having children is suddenly a detriment in our lives, and now, with this woman back in your life with your child, I am understandably nervous." She touched my hand. "I love you. We have such a perfect life together. I don't want anything to change, but this has changed things, and we both need to grow with this. I never want to lose you."

We embraced as I replied, "You'll never lose me. You're stuck with me forever."

"Hey, Beth—long time." I was looking at a woman I hadn't seen in years but had never forgotten. We had become close when Sterling and I were dating, and I had become friends with her late husband, Nicky. Neither pretty nor plain, but unique, with graying hair, Beth had a face that was more severe than I remembered, reflecting a life well lived and much suffered. The journey always takes its toll, and Bethany duPont was no exception. Widowed young by a man who loved to fly but lacked the sensibility and luck to survive, she embodied a self-sufficient woman from a bygone era – calloused, independent, yet soft in her daily joy of life.

"Hi Dags," she replied, coming to give me a sincere hug. "God, when did I last see you?"

"It's been a long time, Beth. Too long," I replied.

She grabbed my hand. "Please, come in. Sterling and Maddie are upstairs packing." She held the door for me as I entered. "How have you been?" she asked, obviously wanting to make me feel at home.

I laughed at the loaded question. "The past several days could have encompassed a lifetime for me, with the spectrum of feelings I've dealt with. I'm guessing you know the whole story."

"I've known about you, my sister, and my niece forever, but does anyone ever know the whole story?" She smiled. "Let's go sit in the kitchen. I've made some sandwiches for everyone."

I followed her from the foyer down the hall and into an open kitchen that looked out over three ponds that stepped down the hill. The view of the countryside coupled with the gray, misty day gave me an inadvertent chill.

"Coffee?" she asked, and I quickly nodded. She poured me a cup and we sat in a comfortable silence, sipping the warmth, until I broke the spell.

"How are your kids doing? Have you been blessed with any grandchildren yet?"

She smiled at a question she probably hadn't answered in years. It's rare to run into old friends you haven't seen in so long that a new generation needs to be discussed.

"Jason just graduated from Delaware and, get this, is taking flying lessons. I'm worried sick over what may happen to him, so I try not to think about it. It's some sort of itch that needs to be scratched in order to find closure with his father, I think. Avery is now twenty-eight, if you can believe that, and has twin four-year-old daughters, Zibi and Zoe. They are the cutest girls, and I spoil them rotten every chance I get."

A movement caught my eye as a pair of swans came circling over. They made a 180-degree turn before settling with a graceful, synchronistic splash, cackling back and forth to each other over the beauty of their landing.

"You've got a gorgeous place here, Beth. I know it's very special to you."

We were interrupted by animated conversation as Sterling and Madeleine entered. I rose and gave each of them a self-conscious, perfunctory hug.

"Good morning, ladies," I said and was rewarded with a "Good morning, Dags" in unison. "Dad" was an endearment that Madeleine might never use, and surprisingly I missed hearing her say it. *Maybe someday.* "Are you packed and ready to go? You might want to call the airlines to see if there are any weather delays."

The women exchanged glances, rolling their eyes and laughing. "Madeleine, I just don't know how we got along without him for so many years," Sterling said. "Thank god he's here to right our foundering ship." After another shared giggle, Sterling looked at me and said, "Yes dear, Madeleine checked, and our flight is going to be forty-five minutes late, probably later. The mist should burn off soon into a partly cloudy day, warming into the low sixties." She turned to Madeleine. "Did I get that right?"

Madeleine gave her mother a mock look of disapproval. "Mom, stop that! You don't want to scare him off so soon, do you? I barely know him."

I was finding this repartee amusing yet somewhat unnerving. The day was off to a great start—first I'd been grilled by my wife, and now I was being mocked by my former lover and our daughter.

To gather myself and deflect any more arrows, I turned to Bethany. "Help me here, Beth; I'm in the middle of an unfair fight."

Bethany smiled and lightly chided the two women. "Here, let's have a sandwich. We need to treat our guest with the respect he deserves."

We sat, we ate, and we laughed, all of it feeling so natural and relaxed. Beth's home was inviting, and my temporary family was doing what families do, enjoying the intimacy of each other's company. I could keep this dream alive if I concentrated on remaining in the present, which I did as I watched my daughter enliven our conversation with her charm and her wit. Sterling had done a magnificent job raising her. And if I do say so myself, I had contributed mightily with my DNA. In short, she couldn't have done it without me, right?

Eventually the sun began streaking through the mist, those streaks broadening as the fog melted away. Madeleine checked the departure time and informed us that it was time to go. Bethany and Madeleine shared a long embrace, each promising not to let so much time pass between visits. Bethany suggested a girls' trip to New York to see a couple of plays and spend too much money at fine restaurants. They agreed and shared some more hugs, and then Sterling and Madeleine got in the car.

When they were in, I walked over to Bethany and embraced her. "Thanks for everything, Beth. Let's keep in touch." There was so much more I wanted to say; I hoped she heard it.

Wanting to prolong my time with Sterling and Madeleine, I followed the historic route from yesterday, hoping I might even get lost. Returning to Route 52, we again were bathed in silence until Madeleine, sitting beside me, began what would become another volley of comments and questions from a female whose company I was thoroughly enjoying.

"I really don't know what to call you. 'Dad' just doesn't work for me right now, and I don't think I know you well enough to call you Dags."

"What do you want to call me, profanities excluded?" I needed to make some connection with her, even if only as a friend of her mother's.

"I don't know. Everything sounds weird."

At least we were talking.

"Then call me whatever you want." The thought *I don't want to piss off the daughter of a deadbeat dad* did cross my mind, was maybe even front and center.

"Okay. Do you like Dagger?" Great! Had my wife somehow channeled her evil powers to my daughter? I knew I was fucked, but Madeleine's next comment surprised me. "I'm really sorry about your buddy," she said.

I looked over at her before returning my gaze to the road. I wasn't prepared for direct honesty. *Damn,* I thought, *she has a little bit of her father in her.* I wasn't sure I liked it.

"Thanks," I replied, wondering where to take this. I had to tell her the truth. "Maddie—is it okay if I call you Maddie?" She nodded. "Dagger's okay as long as you say it with kindness. Clyde was a close friend and a really special guy. Until he got sick, he was my closest friend. After he got sick, he still should have been my closest friend, but I possessed neither the compassion nor the patience to help him, so I pulled away. I don't know if you've heard this, but his last words to me, his last words on this earth, as far as I know, were, 'Dagger, thanks for ruining my life.'"

Every time I said that sentence, every time I thought about that sentence, and every time I thought about Clyde, I experienced temporary shock, my psyche shielding me from the maliciousness of his words. I took a breath, stifling thoughts that were too complex to throw at my daughter.

"Maddie, this was a good guy who was overwhelmed by drugs, and I hastened his end through my ignorance and callousness. I didn't make him shoot himself, but I certainly didn't try hard enough to stop him." I weighed my ensuing feelings carefully before jumping in with a gratuitous comment along the lines of Clyde being a fucking asshole to have done it in the first place. I shouldn't have said it, and Madeleine seemed to ignore it.

"What was he like?" she asked.

"We have a relatively short drive ahead of us," I said. "I don't have the time to fully explain the complexity of our friendship or our estrangement in one sitting. He was my best friend, and there will never be another like him. If you and I develop a relationship, you will hear me speak of him often. I hope we get there."

"Was he married?" she pressed.

I tried again to remember why I had gotten out of bed that morning.

"Yeah, he was married with no children, just like me and my wife, Katy—your stepmother. I hope you meet her someday soon, by the way." I glanced over and smiled; Madeleine reciprocated. I didn't expound on the subject, figuring I didn't need another shovel to help me dig the hole I was now intent on digging. "It was a beautiful service," I added. "He had a lot of friends."

Madeleine seemed to be trying to imagine what Clyde was like—she wasn't going to let go of the subject—and so I really needed to paint my friend in a sympathetic light without showing her the dichotomy of my feelings, something I suspected I'd already done.

"Madeleine, if he had only known how to reach out for help, a thousand hands would have reached back. Clyde was a very complicated man who was always getting into trouble, so his friends would get pissed off at him at times. I'm pissed off at him now. But it never lasted long, and these crazy stories about him will last for years in the retelling. Still, for whatever reasons, he died an isolated man. It's such a tragic story, and I hope something like this never happens again. But it will, to someone." I glanced at her, adding, "I'm sorry for sounding so cynical about this."

We continued on, driving slowly through the evaporating mist, the mood in the car conducive to the languid feel of the early afternoon. I had talked, grieved, and thought enough about Clyde. For the moment I needed to move forward, to escape his death while investigating a future with my daughter. I didn't know how to begin. Should I just start talking, hoping for some fluid direction? Why not?

"Can we talk about our relationship instead of mine with Clyde? Clyde is in a place that is timeless, and we only have thirty minutes to begin our journey as a family. Maddie, I don't want to disrupt what you have with your mom. It's obviously special." I slowed for a curve before continuing. "I want to be in your life. I would like to be a father to you. I want to be a person you can come to for advice and comfort, or simply as a friend. I don't want to do this all at once, but I just want you to know that I love you."

Was I making any sense or simply turning her away? What she already had was perfect. Why fuck with that now? I had low expectations until she replied.

"Dagger—god that sounds so weird—you seem like a pretty good guy, but you don't seem like my father. Maybe you never will. But I'm willing to see where it goes. I've never had a father and never really missed having one, since so many fathers leave, but I would like to continue this story. It's been an interesting weekend"—she glanced at her mother—"to say the least."

"What do you do in Tampa?" I asked.

"I'm working for a nonprofit, interning with some sales personnel as I learn how to coerce money from wealthy people with a conscience. I like it."

A young woman with ideals and a sense of humor? I was so proud!

"Do you like Florida?"

"I haven't known much else. Every place has its faults, but I have a lot of friends there and my mom is close by. Have you ever been to Boca Grande?"

"I would have if I'd known you and your mom were there, but I was never invited." Sterling and I shared a humorous glance through the rearview mirror.

She quickly piped up. "I would have invited you if you had told me where you were." She said it with a smile. I didn't take offense.

Madeleine laughed and said, "Mom, he's driving us to the airport. Be nice." She turned back to me. "Boca Grande is a sleepy island that hasn't changed much since my mother moved there. They've got a fancy resort, the Gasparilla Inn and Club, but it's what you might call casually elegant. It's very quiet, sometimes too quiet, until someone gets married. Then nobody sleeps for days."

Serenity turned to gray chaos as we approached Philadelphia International Airport, one of the many drab-bordering-on-dilapidated airports on the East Coast. The airport contrasted with Madeleine's sunny disposition. How could she be so happy? To begin with, I reminded myself, she was only twenty-three; she bore no scars from adulthood.

We discussed parking the car, but Madeleine insisted that we drop her off. She was an adult, she would see us again soon, blah, blah, blah. That's not really what she was saying, but that's what I was hearing. We pulled to the curb and got out. I watched as the women exchanged such intimate hugs, talking and listening at the same time—a female gift—as I again wondered what might have been. Then Madeleine gave me a hug, whispering, "I'm glad I found my dad." She gave me a quick kiss on the cheek and then turned to go.

Sterling and I stood there, watching her be enveloped by the Philadelphia travelers. Then she was gone, and Sterling and I were alone, having watched our daughter grow up. At least I did. Sterling was simply watching her daughter depart for her flight, as she had so many times before. I had a lot to learn.

"I can't believe what I just did and how I felt."

"Watching your daughter walk away? Get used to it!" Sterling said as she nudged me toward the car. "Let's go for a ride."

"The sun is beginning to shine. Why don't we go for a walk? My aunt still owns some property in Chadds Ford. I'm sure she wouldn't mind."

We parked the car in a little-used gravel driveway, no sign of life from my aunt—and began walking through the woods on a dirt path I had used as a kid. I was always amazed at how some things never change. My grandparents had carved this path for some long-forgotten reason, and it was still here.

I grabbed Sterling's hand, hoping she didn't take it as an affront. Our hands met and our bodies melded into one as our feet explored the peat-scented path.

"You've raised a beautiful daughter, Sterling. I'm a little bit jealous." I chuckled uncomfortably, realizing I was being self-centered; Sterling was gracious enough to ignore the comment. We kept walking.

"You brought me here before, many years ago. Do you remember?"

I nodded, remembering full well how successful I had been bringing her to this secluded spot on a warm, early-summer night so many years before. We approached a clearing and stopped as a surprised groundhog ducked for cover.

Sterling took both my hands in hers and sighed. "The smell today is exactly as I remember it the last time we came here. Do you smell it? God, it's the scent of, I don't know, life, I guess. Do you know what I'm trying to say?"

"Yes, and I couldn't have said it better." I didn't know what else to say, so for once I shut up.

"Every spring you see the beginning of life, but you also see the remnants of the past—the fallen, brown leaves still present after the snowmelt, the broken twigs we kick away as we walk. It's all here in spring, life and death."

I knew what she was trying to do. I dimly remembered that annoying quality Sterling had, one she apparently was still burdened with, from years past: that of forcing me to think, to confront my feelings while prodding and probing to get to the core of my psyche. Basically she used to make me feel like shit because I didn't need or even want to visit the core of my psyche. I didn't even know where to look. Now I still kinda felt like shit, but for a different reason: what she'd said was true. I had that trite religious saying going through my mind, "When God closes one door, another door opens"—i.e., Clyde checks out and Madeleine surfaces. My cynical question was, why must a door close in order for one to open? Couldn't we occasionally have it both ways?

I know, I know—never question God's actions or people speaking about them unless you have a lot of time on your hands and a high tolerance for pain from participating in an unwinnable argument. What Sterling said, though, was true: spring buried the dead and welcomed the newly born. Could I do the same?

We approached the springhouse, an old rundown building where farmers used to garner the water, and stepped through the doorless entry. Some stone benches still remained inside, and so we sat. Sterling looked at me with a demure smile. "'And what are your intentions bringing me here, Mr. Bissell?' the young maiden shyly asked." She gave an exaggerated double blink to feign innocence.

I gently laughed as I drew her close and kissed her, interspersing between kisses signs of my intention to show her the intricacies of love from her valiant knight. That guttural sound again escaped her throat as she began kissing me with a long-forgotten fervor. God, what was I doing—or more important, how long would I be able to do it? I soon had my answer, as Sterling abruptly pulled away.

"Whew!" she exclaimed. "You have overwhelmed this young maiden again." She inhaled deeply and leaned her head on my shoulder. We gently caressed each other, afraid to stop because of the reality of the moment that arrived too soon.

"What might have been, what could have been, cannot be," Sterling mused. "We can't recapture lost magic, Dags, however hard we try. However much we want to, we just can't."

She was right, I knew it, but I wasn't going to let her walk peacefully away without a lighthearted jab. "You sound like you're writing one of your books—'lost magic,' 'might have been.'" I exaggerated a sigh and lightly tickled her ribs.

She pushed me away in mock anger before reaching over, giving me a surprisingly long kiss, and then pushing me away again. I'm easily confused, and she was confusing the hell out of me.

"This is wrong. This is so wrong!" She wasn't even looking at me, but simply staring through a breach in the wall. "You're married, and here we are in some rundown farm shed pretending we're twenty-five years old again. We're not, and we're not single. At least you're not." She turned and looked me in the eyes. "Dags, this promises to be very complicated, simply having you back as Madeleine's father. That is as complicated as I can get."

She pulled me close and kissed me again. It was a kiss that lacked the mania of the last one but showed the intimacy that she felt, a kiss that promised to be her last. She pulled away and cupped my face with her hands. "I have always loved you, and I always will love you. I am so happy to have a piece of you back in my life. I have discovered a long-lost friend, and for that I will always be grateful."

During her revelation, I had become speechless, wondering if she was going to kiss me again. I was disappointed when she didn't, and I remained speechless for a few more moments. Then, trying to break the magic of the moment, I offered, "So you actually think having an affair with your long-lost married lover and the newly discovered father of your child is too complicated? You actually believe that?"

She lightly punched my shoulder with a "You asshole!" mixed in. We laughed and hugged before I did the gentlemanly thing, saying, "Let's walk back to the car. Maybe someday you will write a book about our torrid love affair that wasn't meant to be."

As we walked, Sterling asked me how I was coping with Clyde's death. So much had happened in such a short period of time that I really didn't know how to respond. His poisonous call seemed a lifetime ago, yet it had been only a few days. I had touched on the subject with her the day before, during our drive to Wilmington.

"His doctor called me yesterday, wanting to talk."

Sterling didn't know the specifics, and so I again explained the weed-for-Percocet trade Clyde had been so proud of, going into greater detail about their personal and medical relationship.

"He was trading drugs with a doctor?" she asked, incredulous.

"Yeah, and had been for years. I'm pretty sure they got high together, and that's why he called. I'm hoping to meet him tomorrow. I'd already grown to hate the man, and then when I found Clyde dead, I truly believed I had the motivation to seek revenge. Now, after hearing his voice on the phone, I'm not so sure."

"What do you mean by revenge? Alerting the authorities?"

My troubled look and silence begged for more probing.

"It doesn't mean something more sinister than that, does it, Dagger?"

Sterling stopped and turned toward me, forcing me to meet her gaze. I ignored her and kept walking.

"Does this revenge include murder? You weren't thinking of that, were you?" She caught up with me, this time standing in my path, serious about blocking any additional movement. "Dags, please tell me you aren't serious."

She gently grabbed my chin, and when our eyes met, I felt emboldened, like she was looking into the eyes of a stranger.

"When I saw what was left of my friend—his final, desperate act reaping him the reward of a bullet to his brain, his life over but his body still warm—yes, Sterling, I believed if Sanders had been in that room, I could have killed him. I have fantasized about killing him slowly, and how I might do it. He killed my friend, and he has the power to kill others."

"But now you're not so sure? That's a great awakening, Dags." Sterling was learning that she really hadn't known me for a long time. I could see she was nervous now, having introduced her daughter to a morally ambiguous man. "Dags, stop. You're scaring me. Look at me. This is serious, and I want to see your eyes and your expression when you answer. You're my daughter's father, and I think I deserve an honest answer to this question."

Our final kiss seemed forever lost. The last woman in my female troika was getting her chance to grill me, and making the most of it.

Suddenly I was tired of them all. They demanded so much honesty and thoughtful introspection that I was reevaluating my position in all this and getting a massive headache in the process. I was low human on this totem pole, with no chance for promotion. Why was I suddenly involved with three women?

I met her gaze and said, "In a prurient way, I believe I could protect my family and friends to the point of destroying those trying to destroy me or my loved ones, and do it without remorse."

Sterling's mien was becoming more serious the more I spoke. I knew it was time to tamp it down.

"This is all theoretical. The point is that when I heard the doctor's message, I felt like I was listening to another victim. It was almost like he was taking full responsibility for Clyde's death. My dark fantasy dissipated. And Sterling, it *was* just a dark fantasy, almost a challenge to see if I was brave enough to destroy evil. If someone were attacking Madeleine, what would you do?"

She shot me an exasperated look. "That's completely different and you know it. Instinctively fighting for a life bears no relation to plotting revenge on someone. At the risk of sounding pedantic, I'll just point out that one is self-defense and one is murder. Please tell me you know the difference." She left my side and walked purposefully away.

I guess "That Magic Moment" song that I might have had dancing in my head was toast.

I caught up with her and forced her hand into mine. "Sterling, I'm sorry. I've been really upset at what happened, and I guess I was just lashing out in anger about something that I am partially responsible for. I keep wishing I hadn't made that call to his family. If I don't make the call, he doesn't stick a loaded gun in his mouth, at least not yet. I was the first domino; his trigger finger was the last. You can't imagine what it was like hearing him say what he said. He was so controlled, so to the point. He accomplished exactly what he wanted to accomplish, and fate led me to find him. Shit, I could have just told him to fuck off and gone to bed. Then some other lucky soul, his wife, would have been burdened with discovering his body. But really, it had to be me. The symmetry was too perfect for it not to be me."

I looked away, fighting back tears. Sterling came to me and hugged me like a parent protecting a child. And a child I suddenly became as the tears began to flow freely.

"No, Dags, I'm sorry. I have been so concerned with you and Madeleine that I've neglected the reason we are all here." She hugged me tighter. "I've been scared to ask you for the details. Hearing you tell Madeleine about it gave me chills."

Sterling didn't have Katy's prestige or her accompanying baggage, so I somehow felt freer to talk to her. It was almost like unloading to a psychologist, except one I wanted to sleep with. But then most guys had a thing for their psychologists, didn't they?

I put Sterling the woman on the back burner and again recounted my relationship with Clyde, this time to Sterling the psychologist I wanted to sleep with. As we walked through the damp woods, passing my grandparents' dog cemetery and the barn that had housed Tony the Pony forty years earlier, I spoke of my love for Clyde, my exasperation with Clyde, and ultimately my hatred for Clyde. All she did was listen.

14

I told her everything, beginning with when we were young, and ending by boring her again with the details of his suicide. When I was done, there was nothing more either of us needed or wanted to say. I dropped her at Bethany's, having decided not to come in, and got home just in time for another missed phone call from Merlin Sanders. Katy showed her frustration at me for neglecting to return Sanders's earlier call by handing me the phone with a direct command to call him.

Over the past six years I had come to hate Dr. Merlin Sanders. This was not an impetuous hatred; it was a hatred cultivated as I watched my old friend feed his addictions at the doctor's hands. When I lived far away, I rarely saw Clyde, and so Sanders was never among my primary concerns in life until our annual golf outings, when Clyde would exhibit his ever-growing penchant for meds. Then Sanders, the villain, would raise his ugly head, and my hatred of this unknown man would fester. The more Clyde failed, the more I held Sanders accountable—this stranger, this contemptible magic man.

As I'd so clumsily tried to explain to Sterling, I'd come to the realization that in a theoretical world, I was capable of murder. In a theoretical world, who isn't? I naively believed that we are all capable of killing, that given the right circumstances, any of us would take that sacred human life and extinguish it gladly and aggressively. We are humans—we are at the top of the food chain for a reason—and we will do whatever we need to do to survive. Granted, few of us ever reach that point, but most of us have explored it, or at least some of us. Okay, maybe just me. I say this now because I failed in my explanation to Sterling. She actually thought I might be able to kill someone, so I had to dissuade her of that fact, when in truth I would have relished the opportunity to exact that revenge against a true villain. But when I heard his voice, I suspected Sanders was not the true villain. And yet maybe he was.

Revenge is an elixir of evil, one that should not be taken lightly but should certainly be considered. That journey comes with a price, a price as old as humanity. In 504 BC, Confucius said, "Before you embark on a journey of revenge, dig two graves." Primal hatred is emotional, and emotions run deep, usually trumping rationality. Simply look at the number of people on death row: most of them balanced visceral hatred versus rationality and chose prison and death. The philosopher was right. Whether or not you choose revenge, you should know going in that revenge will take a toll larger than the intended victim. Is that a price you're willing to pay? Know the price, and pay it if you must.

Was I willing to pay that price? Of that I was certain. I could kill that man—too late to save Clyde, but early enough to save others. I had seen Clyde disintegrate with Sanders' help over the years. Now he was dead and I was free to lash out at the man I held responsible. In recent nightmares, I'd envisioned such an opportunity. But how would I do it? Possibilities abounded. Early on, Clyde had told me that Sanders liked to scuba dive, a shared interest of mine, and took many trips to the Caribbean. I could follow him there, maybe hire some women to coerce him onto a boat, and then kill him and feed his remains to the sharks. Shit, when I allow my mind free movement into fantasyland, I never know what I'm going to find, but it's guaranteed to be insane and, most likely, perverted.

Until now, I'd been talking about a faceless villain. Would that change when we met? His earlier phone call had me reevaluating my murderous ideas. Yet he might have been plotting to do away with me, if he already knew that I was aware of his shenanigans. Ah, what a tangled web we weave when plotting revenge.

Now, having heard his voice on my answering machine, I began to question whether I wanted to pay the price of revenge. The man sounded tired and beaten. He sounded frail. He sounded human. He sounded like he too had paid a price for Clyde's death and somehow wanted to commiserate with me. In order for me to fully understand Clyde's fatal addiction, I needed to speak with Merlin Sanders without the Bissell chip on my shoulder and begin to understand him. I checked that chip at the door, took a deep breath, took out my phone, and made the call.

When he answered, I was at a loss for words. The confrontation that I had relished was about to happen, and I was frozen. He said hello, and I said … nothing.

"Hello," he repeated, pulling me from my paralysis and forcing me to respond.

"Dr. Sanders, this is Dags Bissell returning your call." I delivered the line much more smoothly than I thought I would. "I apologize for not getting back to you sooner." This comment assuaged Katy, who retreated back into the house to give me some privacy.

"Thank you for calling, Mr. Bissell. I really appreciate it. Listen, I know Clyde Colson's death is a complicated one for me, and I would imagine it's the same for you."

"It is," I interjected, "for obvious reasons."

Ignoring the comment, he said, "I was hoping you might want to meet somewhere at your convenience to discuss Clyde. You must have some questions for me, and since he has passed away, the doctor-patient confidentiality provision is no longer binding. I live and work in the Philadelphia area. I would be happy to set up an appointment for you at my office or drive down and meet you at a place of your choosing. It would mean a lot to me if you could find it in your heart to help out a failed doctor and a failed friend, Mr. Bissell. Again, I would really appreciate it."

I guess I wasn't going to kill this guy after all, and I couldn't imagine him wanting to kill me. But what did I know?

"Why would I want to talk with someone who helped kill Clyde?" *Be cool, Dagger,* I silently pleaded. *Don't shoot the guy without listening to him.*

"Mr. Bissell, I believe you know this was a lot more complicated than you're implying by accusing me of murder, having known Clyde as long as you did. Can we meet? Please. I really want to talk with you."

He was right. It was a lot more complicated. "Dr. Sanders, I would like to discuss this with you. Can you come to Centreville tomorrow? Do you know Buckley's?"

"Very well." He chuckled quietly, having apparently wasted a good part of his youth at Buckley's as well. "Let me buy you lunch."

After agreeing on a time, I hung up feeling that my recent life consisted of continuously putting out fires as others erupted. I was tired, and Katy was certain to grill me on my afternoon activities—yet another blaze to extinguish—so I went inside to grab a beer and try to relax. That wasn't going to happen.

Katy was at the kitchen table, awaiting the report I didn't know I was supposed to present. She was trying to play relaxed but not pulling it off. That was understandable. When shit got thrown into my stall, she always had to help with the cleanup.

"Do you feel like talking about your afternoon?" she ventured. "If it's too soon, that's okay." She let loose with one of those heartfelt, melting smiles that spoke volumes of her love for me.

"It went okay, but I'm really tired. I'm having lunch with Sanders tomorrow. God, I hope I don't kill him." I gave her an abbreviated chuckle so she understood I was kidding. I didn't want to get metaphorically shot by two women in the same day.

"Would you like me to come with you? Maybe act as a referee?" She laughed, signaling the end of that discussion for the night. "I pulled out some steaks and bought a nice pinot noir. Why don't you go get cleaned up while I fix a cheese plate."

I was home. And I was safe, at least temporarily, so I went upstairs to shower. I took off my clothes and walked to the bathroom. I turned on the shower and looked in the mirror as the water warmed.

Who are you? You look different, I mused as I viewed a man who now seemed like a stranger to me. What was it? The brow was furrowed, the lips drawn taut, but the eyes held the answer to why this stranger was staring back at me. They had darkened, baring the sadness in his soul, the shock of loss and the experience of death. A different man was staring back at me, a man stung by death. That man was now only the two-dimensional shell of a once-vibrant being.

He hung up the phone, took a deep breath, and pinched the bridge of his nose. *What have I done?* he silently mourned. He made his way to the bar and poured a shot of Macallan scotch into a cut-glass tumbler, adding a few drops of water. He began swirling the glass, mesmerized as the color snaked its way up the glass before slowly melting back down. The delicacy of the swirl came to a sudden, violent end as he threw back the shot, almost eliciting a muted scream as the scotch awakened a forgotten vibrancy in his life. Pouring another shot, he again added a couple drops of water, intent on enjoying this drink more than the last. He went to his office and popped in a Bruce Springsteen CD. Then he sat down at his desk, opened the top left drawer, and grabbed a joint, an ashtray, and a lighter.

Merlin Sanders was home too, but he was alone and far from safe—alone to face the consequences of his actions, alone to face those fast-emerging demons he had spent a lifetime trying to tamp down. He opened the opposite drawer. There it lay, his 45 caliber colt single shot American 1911 Commander Pistol, a gift from his father. A single shot was all he had planned, but the magazine held eight bullets. With its mahogany grips and deep-blue and hard chrome finish, it was a collector's item, and dear old Dad hadn't expected it ever to be shot again. But it would be shot again—maybe once, maybe more. Great gift, Dad.

Merlin needed to tie up some loose ends. He was a precise man, so everything he did was carefully analyzed, including his departure. He was not checking out angry, like Clyde; life was too precious. So when his time drew to a close, his departure had to somehow acknowledge that gift.

His life had been a gift. Raised comfortably on the Main Line of Philadelphia, Merlin had nailed prep school, attended Princeton for his undergraduate program, which entailed chasing the Princeton cats, and somehow been accepted to the University of Pennsylvania's Perelman Medical School. After graduating from Perelman in 1984, he started a general practice and was an overnight success. Marriage followed, with two children. The Sanders' family life was the script for American family values—that is, until the script demanded reality. And that reality manifested itself in Merlin's drug use. "The Magic Man" was not a recently invented nickname, but one he had earned at Princeton through his knowledge and dispersal of pharmaceuticals. In short, Merlin was a drug dealer; yet somehow he thrived. Both his consumption and his constitution were prodigious. When he met Clyde, it was a collision of two perfect storms.

Pete Everhart had been the catalyst. The three men—Clyde, Pete, and Merlin—shared common qualities: extreme intelligence, a penchant to get fucked up, and the wherewithal to make money while doing it. For years as their families grew, their lives ran on separate tracks; Pete didn't introduce Clyde to Merlin until all three were in their early forties. One winter after the death of their daughter, Pete and his wife rented a villa in Jamaica and invited Merlin and his wife, along with Clyde and Joanne, to join them for ten days. Pete had known Clyde since childhood, and Merlin since their Princeton days, so the Colsons seemed a natural fit as the third couple. And fit they did. As soon as Clyde landed, he set off to find the world-famous Jamaican *ganja,* an effort that was soon rewarded by a helpful stoned local. "Need the blow, mon, got that too." Clyde was set. Cocaine, ganja, rum, and sun were the ingredients to his perfect concoction for a tropical vacation. Merlin was the Everharts' doctor, so he came supplied with Xanax, Ambien, and Percocet to help them dull their grief. When Merlin saw Clyde's stash and Clyde saw the doctor's bag, their slow dance toward the dragon commenced. By the end of the ten days together, Clyde was the proud new owner of a primary care physician, and Merlin was swimming in weed.

Clyde slowly became an indomitable presence in Merlin's life, and with Merlin's marriage dissolving, Clyde offered him a way to mask the pain he was feeling from the loss. Getting fucked up on weekends with his buddies was the perfect tonic for Merlin until the day Clyde made him an offer that he should have refused—a bag of high-quality weed for one hundred Percocet. The moment he agreed to the swap, he began to compromise his profession and the "Do no harm" tenet he had always tried to follow.

Merlin was caught in the middle of Clyde's spiral, and before he knew it, Clyde was a raging Percocet addict, with the responsibility falling to Merlin to try and figure out how to stem his fall. Merlin had developed an addiction to Percocet but had recognized the symptoms early and was able to overcome it. Pete was not so lucky. Under Merlin's advice, Pete checked himself into a detox center and, later, a rehab facility for several weeks. Clyde's addiction was the most virulent of the three. Merlin was unable to convince Clyde to detox and so held himself accountable for Clyde's fatal shot.

Merlin didn't know what made him call Dags Bissell. Clyde had broad-brushed his friendship with Dags but finely detailed Dags's traitorous phone call. Merlin sympathized with Dags, having seen the rage spewing from Clyde's soul, yet he also hated the man for sticking his nose where it didn't belong. Their friendship had to have been special for both men and now especially hard for Dags after Clyde's rumored malicious phone call. Merlin knew Clyde was suicidal, knew he was fighting depression, and knew depressives often lashed out at family and friends in their darkest moments. He was a depressive himself, having occasionally considered suicide or, in darker moments, murder. A cynical laugh escaped him as he remembered how lucky his ex-wife had been. She didn't have a fucking clue how close she had come to meeting her maker that dark, explosive night when she announced she was leaving and taking the kids with her. Their kids. They had saved their mother's life with their mere presence that night as Merlin's rage nearly overwhelmed him.

A passing cloud shadowed the window, darkening the room and encouraging Merlin's simmering anger to percolate to the surface.

Try as he might, he couldn't control his hatred for Bissell for all the pain he had caused. Not so much for the death of Clyde—that had been predetermined—but for severing the bond Merlin had shared with Clyde and Pete. Their special strength had been the ability to cope together as well as three depressives could. The delicate balance of the three-legged stool had been upset because of Bissell's self-centered meddling in lives he barely knew and did not understand. Now the stool was upended on the floor, one leg missing, another broken. Merlin's life was beginning to disintegrate.

He returned the weed to the drawer, no longer wanting the high, and concentrated on his scotch as he tried to figure out how he'd gotten here, suffering profound regret for virtually everything he had touched over the last ten years. He had been a bad husband and a worse father to two daughters. He had suffered the hubris of early success and corrupted a sacred profession for personal and illegal gain. Clyde had intoxicated him, but his power was no excuse for Merlin's liberal administration of dangerous narcotics.

Merlin took a last sip and moved to the bar for a refill. Another sarcastic laugh escaped him as he poured. He didn't need to figure out how he got here; he knew exactly how he got here, saw it coming several years ago. Every choice he made and every decision he reached was a sham for fun and profit. *Dammit, face it! Own it and get over it! You were complicit in a friend's death. Just admit it. You fucked up.*

Shaking his head, he returned to his desk, sat down, and opened the drawer with the weed. Reconsidering, he lit up the joint, took a long drag, and held his breath until he began to cough violently. Feel the pain; mask the pain. He took another hit with similar results and then opened the drawer with the gun. Another jaded laugh as he realized he was participating in a dance with the dragon that had so recently danced with Clyde.

He removed the gun. The weight and balance were perfection, a deadly work of art. He held the gun in his left hand, unconsciously caressing the handle with his right. One simple move and it would end. No more asshole husband, dirtbag father, or charlatan doctor. Turn the wrist, suck on the steel, touch the trigger, and chew the bullet. Done! Simple. Almost intoxicatingly easy. That was the trap. In the millisecond of the moment between squeezing the trigger and dying, are there regrets? Probably, he thought, before realizing that it didn't matter.

The adrenaline charge had been tempered enough to allow Merlin to replace the gun in the drawer. Today was not going to be his last day—of that he was certain. Maybe tomorrow, but not today.

Monday morning. What happened to Sunday night? Probably the same thing that had happened every night since Clyde killed himself: alcohol, guilt, hatred, the run-of-the-mill emotions, and the drugs I used to move another day away from Clyde's shot. This was not going to be easy. Jack could massage the truth with his eulogy, and friends could brainwash me into thinking Clyde was being twisted when he called, but the reality was that he tried to take me out with him—he tried to kill me. I lay in bed, thinking, *What an asshole!* Great way to start the day.

Monday morning. Lose the past and concentrate on today. Today I will have lunch with my friend's killer, maybe too harsh an assessment, maybe not. After all, I, too, could be construed as a complicit partner. Just ask Joanne.

I rolled over; again, no Katy. I dimly remembered something from last night about yoga and shopping with the girls. She was giving me space, allowing me to figure things out about Clyde, Sterling, and Madeleine, while keeping a safe distance from my maelstrom.

Jack was coming by in a couple of hours to give me a pep talk and pat me down for any firearms I might want to smuggle into Buckley's. I hadn't seen him since the service and wanted him to realize what his message had meant to me.

First things first, though—another eye-opening, hangover-erasing shower. I may have been damaged from Clyde's suicide, but at least I was keeping clean. Was I showing signs of OCD, or simply reenacting a Shakespearean tragedy? Or was "Out damn'd spot! Out, I say!" Lady Macbeth merely showing medieval signs of OCD as she vainly scrubbed the imaginary blood of King Duncan from her hands? Did I have blood on my hands, and were all these showers my modern attempt to cleanse my guilt? Was Sanders feeling that same guilt? There were too many uncomfortable questions for me to sanely answer so I entered the shower and began to scrub.

Jack walked in without knocking as I was finishing a late breakfast. Other than the same frame, mannerisms, and voice tonality, I saw none of the brotherly similarities between us that the rest of the world seemed to recognize—yet another great example of everyone being wrong except me.

"You need to get outside, Dags," Jack began before adding with a smile, "You look like shit."

"Thanks for your concern." I laughed and turned to the fridge. "A couple of waters, coffee, juice, maybe a scotch?"

Jack chuckled. "Water is fine. Let's go sit on your patio. The weather guru is calling for record-breaking heat in the seventies. It's beautiful, Dags, a great day to be alive."

His positive spin was not lost on me as we made our way outside to the morning sunshine. The late morning was still crisp, and one invigorating breath confirmed Jack's assessment: it truly was a great day to be alive.

"Too bad Clyde couldn't see his way clear to fight a little harder to live," I replied as we drank from our water bottles.

Jack sat back for a moment, thinking. "You know, Dagger, there are certain people in this world that, when you really think about it, you know are going to die an unnatural death. Whether it's from hard living or extreme risk taking or even depression, we have known people who were destined to die young. I think we both understand that Clyde was one of those guys. You said yourself the last time you saw him that he looked like he was about to die of a heart attack. You were concerned and reached out to his family. You did the right thing; it just didn't work out the way you had hoped, the way it should have." He shifted around in his chair to look directly at me. "You can't blame yourself for what happened. He might have collapsed from a heart attack or died in a car wreck, killing someone else along the way, and then you would have been wracked with guilt for not having tried. His death is a great loss for us all, so try to concern yourself with that and not his phone call."

I didn't meet his eyes, instead concentrating on some crocus buds beginning their cycle early. "It was a clumsy attempt on my part, and I should have risen above his hatred for me and tried a little harder to help him. I realize that now, but now it's too late. Only a select few knew he was suffering from depression, and we weren't among them. You're right, though, about his dying young. No one believed he would live a long life, but I hate that he checked out so pissed off." I took another long swig from the water bottle before continuing, this time looking at him. "Jack, your eulogy was so heartfelt and so sincere, you even had the balcony crying. You've always possessed the gift of discovering people's assets while ignoring their failings. Clyde had an abundance of both." We laughed, and he thanked me as we returned our gaze to spring's awakening.

After a moment, I ventured, "Do you remember my old girlfriend Sterling Rodgers?"

Jack nodded. "She was quite the dish, as I recall. Why? Have you seen her recently?"

I nodded.

"How does she look now?"

"She's now a middle-aged dish, but to me she hasn't really changed."

I think that got Jack's attention. "So ... that's an interesting segue, seamlessly gliding from Clyde's death to a babe from your past. Where did you run into her? Are you having an affair?"

"She was at the service and happened to sit next to me with her daughter. And no, I'm not having an affair."

"Did you introduce her to Katy?" Jack asked with a grin. Another wiseass in the Bissell family.

"Katy didn't attend the service, but I did tell her about Sterling." I returned my gaze to the crocus buds before continuing. "Turns out Sterling's daughter is mine. As in, I am suddenly a father." I paused to gauge the effect. Timing is everything, and the pause allowed Jack to examine this scenario from multiple angles. I interrupted his thoughts with "Hey, Uncle Jack, you have a new twenty-three-year-old niece. I would be honored if you would be her godfather."

He ignored the comment. "You didn't know about this?"

I shook my head.

"Why didn't she tell you before now?"

I shrugged. "Long story."

"You have been a busy boy this week. Is there anything else I need to know? Are you going to play nice with Sanders today? Where are you meeting him?"

"Buckley's," I replied. "I wanted someplace comfortable and public where I felt safe from any untoward actions from either of us."

"Smart move. When are you meeting?"

"Twelve thirty."

"Would you like some company?"

"Are you scared I'm going to try and kill him? Sterling, Katy, and now you have all offered. I think showing up with my entourage might spook him. What do you think?"

He ignored my sarcastic comment. "Can I witness from a neighboring booth?" he asked, laughing. "Please, Dags, oh please?"

"No, I'm flying solo on this. But thanks for your concern. Oh, and I'll be watching the doors in case you try to crash."

Buckley's is a favorite locals' tavern in the village of Centreville, a few miles north of Wilmington. The building itself dates back to 1817, when it was built as a private residence, and it's been a taproom since the 1930s. The two-story structure was built as a modified T, with white clapboard siding and two dormers overlooking Kennett Pike. Dennis Buckley bought it in 1951, gave it his name, and ran it until 1970, when he sold it to a couple of duPont family members who likely wanted a familiar place where they could drink and charge friends for the privilege of their company. Many generations, including mine, have misspent much of our youth at Buckley's. When we moved from Wyoming, Buckley's was the first tavern I showed Katy, and I ran into a couple of long-lost friends there who may have never left. Apparently, Sanders had occasionally enjoyed the Buckley's ambience as well, so the choice for our lunch was mutually acceptable.

I arrived early, parked the car, and walked in to secure a table, nodding at a couple of acquaintances along the way. The interior had dark paneled walls and a rich, L-shaped bar with tables surrounding it. I chose a table by the door. I didn't know what Sanders looked like, but I was relatively certain I could identify him when he entered. He'd be the single guy, my age, suffering from the same gut shot.

I was right. Ten minutes later, a single man walked in wearing a disheveled coat and tie. His slightly graying hair was moderately long and somewhat unkempt. I motioned him over and introduced myself, praying that I would be cool and not scare him off with any belligerence.

"Mr. Bissell, thanks for meeting with me." Sanders was obviously nervous. Was I as obvious about it?

"Dags. Call me Dags."

"Merle. Good to meet you." We shook hands.

"Beer?" He nodded, and I motioned for two Stella drafts.

Both of us were withdrawn, not wanting to open up until assessing the foe. At least that's how I felt as I tried not to reach over and rip his fucking head off. *Down boy! Get hold of yourself! If you rip his fucking head off at Buckley's, Katy will be really pissed.*

The beers arrived, none too soon, and I returned to reality while waiting for Sanders to begin the conversation. He didn't let me down.

"Mr. Bissell, Dags …" He hesitated and took a breath. "Didn't Clyde call you Dagger?"

"He did," I replied, wondering whether Sanders was procrastinating or trying to make me feel at ease. "Clyde actually reincarnated an old childhood nickname one night when he saw me shoot daggers with my eyes at some asshole who was moving in on my girlfriend.

Somehow the name stuck, and I say that sarcastically, because he made a point of reliving the story with any friend or acquaintance who would listen. We soon discovered that the nickname also kept fellow drug dealers off balance, maybe wondering if I was adept with a knife, which I wasn't. Anyway, we're not here to discuss college history, are we, Magic Man?"

"So you know mine, as well—something I'm no longer proud of. And no, we're not here to discuss history." I saw a flicker of cold anger in his eyes—gone as quickly as it had appeared, but confirmed when he spat, "If you don't cut your sarcastic shit, I'll walk out of here right now."

"Then go. You called this meeting, not me. I didn't agree to meet you in order to hear an apologist squirm out of his role in Clyde's suicide. So you can either leave, or you can calm your ass down and get to the point." My long-lost daggers had suddenly emerged to pierce Sanders's eyes, apparently with the desired effect.

He took a healthy swig of beer. "Please give me a chance to explain myself. This is hard for me to say, and I'm sorry for my outburst, but I want you to know that I had an inadvertent hand in leading Clyde to suicide. I believe you already know that, which is why we're really here, but I needed to tell you that right away."

I was speechless, stunned. This doctor had just admitted to killing Clyde. Maybe that was too strong, but I went with it anyway.

"I want to fill you in on my relationship with Clyde leading up to last week and then answer the questions you are sure to have, if that is okay."

"That is not quite okay," I barked. "First, I have a burning question that needs an answer."

The cold steel returned to Sanders's eyes as his jaw began clenching and unclenching, much like a predator's before the kill.

I immediately backed off, pleading with myself to calm down, and followed his lead with a swig of beer before apologizing. "Sorry, we've all been under a lot of pressure. Before you continue, though, I want to know one thing. Did Clyde trade you a bag of weed for a hundred Percocet?"

The inquisition had begun.

Sanders looked over at me, obviously surprised by the question. He took another swig to gather himself. "Yes, a few times. He must have told you."

"He did," I said. "He bragged about it, thinking I would be impressed. Needless to say, I was so unimpressed. You're a fucking doctor! How could you do that to him? Why couldn't you help him instead of trying to kill him?" I could barely contain my rage with this man. The waitress approached to take our order, and so I quickly regained control of my emotions.

We ordered another round of beer with our sandwiches—mine a simple BLT, lightly toasted with extra mayo, while Sanders went with egg salad on wheat—although neither of us was the slightest bit interested in eating after our outbursts.

Sanders regained his composure and, after a few moments, continued his story. "I have tried to rationalize my motives in accepting his trade." He shook his head and laughed. "His weed was exceptional, so I fogged my principles to accommodate him with the Percocet. I didn't know him well enough to see where this would eventually lead. My wife had left me; I suppose I was feeling somewhat self-destructive. And Clyde, as you must know, was a giant of a personality. It was easy to be pulled into his program."

We were interrupted by the waitress, who brought us our beer and said our sandwiches would be right out. She had a friendlier look to her now that we seemed to have calmed down. We thanked her, and then Sanders continued.

"Let me bore you for a moment with some medical foundation. Percocet abuse begins with feelings of euphoria, and as you may know, the body builds a tolerance to the drug as the abuse—or even simply the extended use—continues, and the user needs to increase the dose in order to achieve the same effects. When a patient has been prescribed Percocet for an extended period of time, the physician must carefully wean the patient from the drug. This is often accomplished with a multiple drug cocktail, so to speak, depending on the severity of the addiction."

Sensing my boredom, which was bordering on frustration, Sanders held up his hand as a plea for patience. He didn't know me very well.

"Bear with me, please," he chided. "This is a meeting to clear some air. Vilify me later, but for the time being, at least give me an opportunity to explain my role."

I looked at him, blinked, and said nothing. I had already waded into enough shit.

We were interrupted again as our lunch arrived. After the waitress walked away, Sanders resumed his monologue.

"The cocktail I ultimately prescribed to Clyde was Librium for his anxiety; Doxepin as an antidepressant; a Catapres patch for his jitters, shakes, and chills; and Ambien to help him sleep at night."

"Helluva cocktail, Doc," I blurted out, immediately realizing what an immature asshole I was being. "I'm sorry," I said. "Go on."

"Unfortunately, it didn't work for Clyde. I'd recognized the early signs of Percocet addiction in myself and had managed to lay off the drug with minimal effort. By the time I realized my own addiction, another friend of ours had reached the same place but couldn't overcome it. He checked into a detox center followed by rehab and has succeeded, so far. Clyde was a different story." Sanders paused, tears beginning to pool. "I helped create this party, and for that reason I will carry his death with me for the rest of my life."

He paused, seeming to struggle for words. "Clyde had to have been doctor shopping or taking trips to pill mills, most likely in Florida. I wrote him an abundance of prescriptions, but not enough to get him to where he was last week. I stopped a long time ago and instead began treating his depression, which was certainly caused by my liberal and unethical behavior." He paused to take a bite of his sandwich.

I needed some levity. "How's your sandwich?" I asked.

He smiled sadly. "About as good as yours."

We ate in silence. Christ, I hated this man; he'd killed my friend. Shit, was he any worse than me when I was younger, selling drugs to strangers and probably causing some of them to become addicted, maybe even die? He wrote the scripts on a pad of paper, while I explored underground networks for illegal drugs. Was either of us any worse than the other? In my apologetic mind, absolutely! The physician has sworn to follow the Hippocratic Oath, to uphold his profession and do no harm. The man across from me had failed miserably at following that oath. Yet here he was in the lion's den, attempting to answer questions about an indictable offense to a man he knew held him responsible. Darkly admirable, I thought.

After another sip of beer, Sanders continued. "I grew quite close to Clyde over the years. The longer I knew him, the more I regretted my decisions to trade with him and supply him with medication. When I realized what I had unleashed, I began to slowly alter our relationship from friends back to doctor and patient. While we were friends, though, he couldn't talk enough about his love for you and your family." He paused, seeming to weigh how to proceed. "And frankly he was devastated when you called his brother. He told me it was like a knife through his heart. He may have even used the word *dagger.* Knowing by then where he was with his drug abuse, I tried to paint you as a concerned friend who might have stumbled in your approach to his addiction, but with good intentions. He wouldn't accept that explanation and went on a self-abuse rampage. I witnessed it and was powerless to help."

He drained his glass, as did I. I motioned to the waitress for two more. Sanders's words were harsh, but I needed to hear them. Finally, someone from the other side was being open and truthful about Clyde's final months.

When the beers arrived, I nearly drained mine in anticipation of the remainder of his story. Sanders took another bite of his sandwich and set it down. "After his family bought him out of their business, he experienced a temporary rejuvenation for life, but that was short-lived, as he became consumed with hatred toward his father and brother. He also felt a profound sense of loss for you, his greatest friend, and everyone connected to you. He never reconciled that loss with me, as I became his caregiver, both medically and psychologically, and was dreadfully inept at both. I recommended a trusted psychologist, and I certainly recommended that he detox, but when he refused both, I was left with no choice but to treat him myself. I couldn't turn my back on him. I am sorry to say this, but he felt isolated because everyone else had turned their backs on him."

I interrupted. "All his true friends would have reached out to help had we known the severity of his illness. Granted, he hated me. I understand that. But he chose to walk away from everyone else. My brother repeatedly tried to talk with him, and others tried as well. He chose that path of isolation; we didn't. He left us, so please don't shift the guilt by altering the truth. The truth is that he ditched the people who really cared so he could hang out with the ones who supplied him with drugs or abetted his behavior: his wife, Pete Everhart, and you. Joanne could have called my brother and asked for help; Jack had been a great friend of his, but Clyde ditched him simply because he was my brother. None of us knew Clyde was depressed until he killed himself. But you knew and did nothing. I've wrestled with the idea of reporting you.

Sanders's look of resignation pulsed anger at my comment, virtually gone before I noticed. Then reflecting his frustration at not being able to break through my rage, he tried again. "That was simply his perception. Clyde told me many times how much you meant to him. He thought the emotion he was feeling was hatred, but it wasn't. What he hated was the sudden loss of your friendship, not you. But he lashed out at you in the end, basically asking, 'How could you?' Many of his friends probably hate him now for killing himself, but again, what they hate is the sudden loss. He cut off everything and everyone with a connection to you because he didn't want any reminders of his loss. He was quite childish that way, very black and white, with an inability to recognize any nuance to the situation."

He paused for another bite and a sip of beer. "You must remember that he was dealing with an insidious addiction that was consuming most of his energy. He told me repeatedly about a dragon-like creature that would lurk in the recesses of his bedroom, an obvious hallucination that overwhelmed him almost nightly. He would be trying to sleep and would hear a noise. This fire-breathing creature would slowly glide, almost dance, toward him with nothing but malevolence burning in its eyes. When the creature was about to kill him, he would scream and awaken in a panic, covered in sweat. We all experience nightmares, but his nightmare was recurring almost on a nightly basis, robbing him of the rest that he so needed. He was perpetually exhausted, making it impossible to fight his depression, and he began to mentally break down as his depression strengthened." He paused and looked at me. "I'm sure you are aware that he came from a family of addicts and alcoholics."

I nodded.

"At the risk of sounding didactic, please allow me to continue."

Again, I nodded.

"Addiction comes in many forms. For example, alcoholism has many strains, some more virulent than others. One family may display mild forms where all the family members drink—quite often a decent amount, and certainly every day—and they may live their lives showing no ill effects from their consumption. Another family might be so genetically predisposed to alcoholism that each member fights a lifelong battle against it. That battle for abstinence may succeed, or it may end in death from alcohol poisoning.

"I say this not just from studying the problem but also from experiencing it. When I was younger, I knew an Irish family with five children. Two of the boys were actually Irish twins, born in the same year. The younger brother struggled mightily with drinking until one day he basically said, 'The hell with it,' sat down with several bottles of vodka, and drank until he died. When he was found a few days later, his apartment was littered with empty vodka bottles and nothing else. When I called the older brother to offer my condolences, he told me that he too had struggled with alcoholism. For him, every day was a battle—a battle he sometimes lost, leading to a stint in rehab. I believe he said he had rehabbed fifteen to twenty times. He told me that his brother's form of alcoholism was more virulent than his, and that his was more virulent than most."

At this point the waitress approached and asked if everything was okay. Suddenly thirsty, I asked for a couple of waters, testing the virulence of my own drinking.

Sanders smiled. "You make light of many serious subjects."

"It keeps me sane," I replied, shooting him my Groucho Marx wild-eyed crazy-guy look.

He shot me another smile before continuing. "Anyway, as you know, Clyde's family was full of addictive personalities, with Clyde's form of addiction being unbreakable. I am not distancing myself from my role in this when I say that had he simply been an alcoholic, I am quite certain that he would have died from drinking, maybe in circumstances similar to those of my Irish friend." He thought for a moment before adding, "Or maybe from lung cancer or heart disease from smoking. Whatever he touched, he craved."

When the water arrived, I took a long, sustaining drink and asked the waitress for some more. I think I was confusing her.

"Did you ever try to help him stop smoking?" I asked. "The last time I saw him, his face was beet-red."

"I was pathetically unsuccessful with any habit suppressions, so ultimately I resorted to damage control: blood pressure medicine, the various drugs for his Percocet addiction, and then antidepressants, which seemed to have a negative effect. His Percocet abuse was the direct cause of his depression, of that I am certain. Toward the end, he isolated himself from me. I later heard he'd had a shotgun taken out of his mouth a few weeks before his suicide. As a friend, had I known this, I would have been proactive in getting him help at any cost. Whoever removed that gun from his mouth should have considered an aggressive form of therapy for him."

"Joanne and Pete?"

"I have a doctor-patient relationship with them both, so I need to concentrate only on Clyde and myself," he replied. "Clyde experienced every trigger for clinical depression. He experienced grief from losing loved ones—you, your brother, and others who cared. Those losses caused social isolation. He lost his job and, with it, any sense of contribution to his family or society. He suffered relationship conflicts—again with you and yours, but also with his family—which deprived him of whatever security he had enjoyed before. These are all symptoms that anyone can find on the Internet, but the most obvious, the most slap-me-in-the-face obvious, is the insertion of a shotgun into his mouth by his own hand. What were they thinking? That he was simply crying for attention?"

Sanders was showing emotion that had been absent in the lead-up to his diagnosis of Clyde. He was clearly upset. He pinched the bridge of his nose and drank some water. I did the same, suddenly wanting to be anywhere but there. Sanders had said enough, but I still wanted to know more.

"How exactly does a guy doctor shop or buy drugs from pill mills on a consistent basis?" I asked.

Sanders was silent, thoughtful, before snapping out of his apparent dream and answering, "Once I began treating his depression with anything but Percocet, Clyde could have easily found another doctor. Basically, he could have walked into a doctor's office or a clinic in Florida and complained about his shoulder; he had a partially torn rotator cuff from a fall on ice a while ago. The doctor would have ordered an MRI that would have shown the tear. No doubt he would have recommended physical therapy or an operation, and in the meantime, he could have been coerced into a couple of Percocet prescriptions—or more, if the doctor was a liberal writer.

"The pill mills in Florida, mostly in south Florida but more recently in Jacksonville too, are overtly illegal cash operations where a patient either brings an MRI with him or gets one on the premises. With the torn rotator cuff, Clyde could have made one trip a month and purchased two hundred to three hundred pills. Remember, when his family forced him out, they paid him well for his exit. With his strong addiction and a lot of money, this was an easy avenue. This is all conjecture, however, because I was no longer in that loop. Have you approached Joanne?"

"I hope to never see that fucking bitch again," I spewed, surprised by my own rage. "She accused me of killing him the night that he died. I'd found him and was calling the police as she was walking into the house. The fact that we are both still alive is a miracle. So, to answer your question, no. I have not and will not speak with either her or Everhart again."

"I'm sorry. I didn't know those details."

We had mutually reached the conclusion of our lunch. Sanders paid the check, leaving a generous tip to cover whatever vulgarity the waitress was sure to have overheard, and we walked back out into the beautiful day. I turned to say good-bye and ask one more question: "How can you live with yourself?"

He studied me for a while, and I saw the darkness in his eyes return before he turned to leave. As he reached his car, he looked back at me, subtly shaking his head. "That's a challenge I'm not sure I can conquer," he said. "I wish you a better fate than mine." Then he was gone.

16

I sat in my car—head against the headrest, eyes closed, breath barely audible, wondering again how I had reached such a place. Sanders's sudden flashes of anger didn't jibe with his patient, thoughtful, and courteous disposition. "Rogue" was the description that came to my mind just before the vibration of my cell phone arrested that thought. It was Sterling.

Without saying hello, I remarked, "Your timing is as impeccable as I always remembered."

"Are you still at Buckley's?"

"Just got finished. I'm relaxing in my car in the parking lot, smoking a joint and getting my shit together after an interesting lunch with Sanders. Just kidding about the joint."

I heard a short laugh on the other end. "You're a funny guy. I'm glad you're still alive. Is he?"

"I wanted to kill him a couple of times, as I'm sure he did me, but I held off so I wouldn't piss off any family or friends. He just left—dispirited, probably pissed, but in one piece. Are you at your sister's?"

"Yes. Beth is out shopping, so I have the house to myself. Would you like to come over and play?" Another giggle. I again realized that she was a shameless flirt, even at fifty.

Ten minutes later I was pulling up in the semicircular driveway.

She met me at the door with a kiss that was surprisingly short for the sensuousness and the sexuality it elicited. The intimacy of the kiss scared the hell out of me, but I welcomed that kind of fear. Acting the brave soul that I strove to be, I returned the kiss. This time she did not pull away. I walked her back into the house, kicking the door closed behind me. As the door latched, the kiss became ever deeper. We moved to a living room couch, never relinquishing our embrace, and began fumbling with each other's clothes. We were young again, in a time warp where the present was everything and everything else was meaningless. We were nearly naked when the sound of a car pulling into the driveway shocked us back to reality.

"Shit! Beth's home," Sterling cried with an odd smile on her face. "Get dressed." She grabbed her pile and fled to the powder room around the corner, leaving me with my … oh, never mind. Let's just say I had about twenty seconds to rally and dress.

Twenty-five seconds later, Beth appeared, having come through the back door. Whew! I was casually standing by a window overlooking her ponds, fully clothed and attempting to capture some of the serenity I was witnessing in the landscape. With a practiced nonchalance, I turned and, as casually as I could manage, said, "Hey Beth, I didn't hear you come in. Sterling is in the powder room. I dropped by for a surprise visit to fill her in on my lunch at Buckley's today."

"Dags, you're always welcome here. Please know that."

She approached for a perfunctory hug. I hoped she didn't catch a whiff of Sterling's scent, which no doubt covered much of my upper body. If she did, she graciously ignored it.

The muffled flush of a toilet signaled that Sterling was presentable. She appeared from around the corner, feigning surprise at Bethany's presence.

"Hi," she said, showing that radiant smile I had fallen for years ago. "I thought you were shopping."

"I was going to return a skirt to the Lemon Drop—it wasn't quite right—but I forgot to take it with me, so I did a couple of errands and just came back home. Stupid me! I hope I wasn't interrupting."

"Don't be silly. Dags just got here and was going to fill me in on his lunch with Clyde Colson's doctor. I don't think he would mind having you listen in"—Sterling turned to me with a sly smile—"would you?"

I'd never learned to say no to her, so why start now? "Beth, if you can stand the boredom, I would like you to stay. All the doc did was admit that he was grossly negligent in treating Clyde and that his negligence played a role in Clyde's death. It doesn't change the outcome, but it made me feel better for a moment."

"He admitted that?" they both exclaimed simultaneously.

"Up front. Pretty much the first words out of his mouth after a not-so-subtle warning to keep my wiseass remarks to myself. So we spent the next hour drinking our lunch while we hashed out who was guilty, with me throwing my guilt onto him, which he was noble enough to accept."

"So you're drunk from lunch?" Sterling asked, shooting me an arrow no man could withstand.

I returned the arrow with a grin and a shrug.

Bethany obviously caught the vibe. "I'll just grab the skirt and be off. Always good to see you, Dags. Please stay in touch. Sterling, I won't be long."

A hint? Regardless, the spell was broken.

Sterling approached me with a softer stance and touched my hand. Once again we viewed the awakening of spring through the picture window, sharing an unspoken bond.

She squeezed my hand and said, "Now, where were we?" She was relentless in her flirting.

My judgment became clouded even as I silently repeated my mantra, *Be strong, be hard*. Hard I was; strong I was struggling with.

"About to do something irretrievably stupid," I replied, not relinquishing her hold. "Let's sit and talk about a few things."

That brought on another glint and a simple question—"Should we sit at the table or on the couch?"—followed by her exaggerated innocent-maiden look.

I led her to the couch and began talking, not allowing her the chance to lighten the moment.

"My lunch with Sanders has made me reevaluate my position in Clyde's death. I realized that I was on the offensive with him, aggressively attacking him in order to somehow distance myself from my involvement in his misadventure." I rose and walked back to the picture window overlooking the ponds. Sterling followed. The soon-to-be-mating swans were still there, as peaceful in their existence as I was overwrought in mine. I watched as they effortlessly moved over the water.

"I have been so consumed by Sanders that I forgot my participatory role. Over the coming weeks, or months, or even years, I'm going to need to confront my own complicity. I really don't give a shit what anyone says, I'm not blameless in this. There are so many things I could have done better. I could have been a better friend. I could have shown more compassion about his addictions and his problems. I should have ignored his addled outbursts and run to help him." I turned to face Sterling, tears welling in my eyes. "I fucked up. Sanders may have aided and abetted, but I applied the coup de grâce."

Sterling gave me a nurturing hug. "Honey, this wasn't your fault," she said. "You tried the best you could at the time. Twenty-twenty hindsight has no benefit in this situation. Interventions rarely go well and are not without conflict and anger. This one was no different. You can't keep beating yourself up over this, or you will end up a victim as well. Dags, you tried to help him. You didn't pull the trigger. He did."

Regaining some composure, I replied, "Unless it's family and I can be present, I'm out of the intervention business. Someone else can do it. I'm not very good at it."

As I took a deep breath, two Canada geese approached the pond and tried to land. The swans flapped their way toward them and drove them away, with the geese settling in on the neighboring pond. It took a few moments for the cacophony to die down, allowing me to broach an entirely different subject.

"How was Madeleine's flight home?" I hoped Sterling would intuit my reason for asking such a simple question.

She responded by taking my hand and leading me downstairs to a back door that opened onto a covered porch. She flipped a wall switch and the enclosure began to retract, leaving us an unobstructed view of the swans and, farther down, the geese. She gestured for me to sit on the cushioned, wooden swing that sat near the front edge of the porch. Then she went to the wet bar and brought back a beer for me and a chardonnay for herself.

"If you spent the day drinking, I need at least one to catch up," she said. "Maddie's flight was fine, and she said to say hi. We spoke for quite some time last night. Mostly about you."

"May I ask if any good things were spoken and, if so, which ones might bear repeating?"

Laughing, she replied, "Many good things were spoken about you, by both of us. But as you probably suspect, it's a little more complicated than that. Not surprisingly, she doesn't resent you for not being there for her, because she and I have such a complete relationship. I don't know if she mentioned this to you, but she doesn't want to upset what she and I have, so inviting you into our family, even if only peripherally, may cause some problems. I suspect that inviting Madeleine into your family may cause similar problems. These things simply need to be worked out with a little effort over time."

Now it was Sterling who stood up and walked a few steps away to gaze out at the woods. "Bethany had it all here: a wonderful, complete family with a beautiful home in an amazing place. Then her husband went out and accidently killed himself. She was never the same; the scar never healed. She raised her children as well as a suddenly single mother could do, but she was incapable of allowing herself to get close to a man, lest she experience the same pain again. They were so in love, and had been since early high school. Beth was angry for a very long time and, to this day, may have yet to forgive him. She learned that too much money can buy dangerous toys that can suddenly kill, and planes are the primary culprit.

"On the other hand, I made the conscious choice to go it alone with Madeleine. I have occasionally regretted my decision but have always felt strong having made it. Who knows if I ever would have discovered my creativity had I married? The guys who walked in and out of my life never possessed the necessary attributes to be the parent I expected them to be. I guess in my romance novel imagination, I was always looking for another you." She turned toward me before continuing, "I knew it only happened in stories, but that was what I wanted. If you never showed, then it made the choice easy." She laughed. "Weird, isn't it?"

I didn't know what to say. The guilt, the yearning, the time lost, my own marriage that was being so severely tested—they all contributed to my being incapable of a reply, and so I let her continue.

She walked over to me. "Dags, I never stopped loving you. I didn't know that until I saw you at the funeral, but it's true. I so want you to be a part of our lives, but if that happens, we can't be carrying on like this. For the sake of our daughter, we need to act like responsible adults." She laughed again, adding, "That was close. Beth may have saved the day with her return."

I'm not sure "saved the day" is the phrase I would have used, but I understood the "responsible adults" phrase a little better. I guess it was time for me to grow up. I moved about the porch, feeling uncomfortable about everything, until Sterling applied the kicker.

She walked over to me and softly took my hand in hers. "With that in mind, I have decided to leave tonight. I have a six-fifteen flight to Fort Myers. We are far too dangerous together in the same town, and I really do need to see how Maddie is doing. Too much has happened to us, to Maddie, to me, and especially to you and your wife these last few days with Clyde's death, and I simply think it's time for some separation and introspection."

That annoying habit of examining feelings had never left her, but I forged on, saying, "Let me take you to the airport." I turned to face her, flashing what I hoped was an irresistible smile. "I don't know when I will see you again, if ever."

"You'd better see us again. You're not running away this time; I simply won't stand for it. If I have to bring Madeleine to you, I will. Do you understand?"

I nodded; she smiled.

"Beth has offered to drive me, but if Katy doesn't mind, I could stand another ride with you. I need to leave in a couple of hours, though."

"Let's plan on it. I'll go home, let Katy know you're leaving, and be back." A quick kiss and I was out the door and headed home.

Katy again met me at the door with the phone in her hand and exasperation on her face.

"Where have you been?"

"Having lunch with Sanders," I replied quizzically. "Why? What's wrong?"

"How can you be having lunch with him when he is calling here?" Katy shoved the phone into my hand and went inside. Her back was still to me when she began, "You're hiding something from me, and I think her name is Sterling." She burst into tears and went to the kitchen. I quickly followed and found her sitting at the table, staring at nothing. I sat down next to her and took her hands in mine. I had some explaining to do—some, but not all.

"Katy, honey, I had a long lunch with Sanders, and then Sterling called to say she was leaving tonight. I've offered to drive her to the airport." I was finally beginning to appreciate Katy's predicament. "Katy, Sterling and I need to figure some things out regarding Madeleine. "This week has been very hard on both of us. When I get back tonight, I'll explain everything, but what needs no explanation is the unconditional love I feel for you. That will never change, and beginning tomorrow, our life together will be a lot less confusing."

Katy finally met my gaze and gave me a self-conscious smile. "I feel like I've been left out of every loop since Clyde died," she said. "I know I should have accompanied you to his service. A good wife would have done that to support her husband, so I'm feeling quite guilty about that. Had I gone, I could have met Sterling and your daughter, and I wouldn't have found them so mysterious and intimidating. I guess I'm just angry at myself and laying it all on you. My naïveté has bitten me again."

She rose from the table and came up behind me, draping her arms around my shoulders and nuzzling my neck with her face. God I hoped she didn't smell Sterling! After a moment she gave me a gentle pat, saying, "Drive safely, but call what's-his-name before you go. He sounded pretty desperate and mentioned something about Clyde."

17

Merlin Sanders arrived home from Buckley's having spent the previous twenty minutes fuming over his mistreatment at lunch. He'd been feeling depressed as he pulled out of the parking lot, but after a few moments, he'd seen what was really happening. Bissell had deflected his own guilt onto himself, making him out to be the bad guy. *Fucking asshole!* Sanders thought. *Who the fuck is this guy?* It was Bissell's phone call that had ruined it for everybody. Now Clyde was dead and Joanne Colson was probably nervous, thinking her Magic Man might go away and take his prescription pad with him. He could see her turning into a major pain in the ass.

He opened the garage door and drove in, closing it behind him. He didn't move; he just sat there in the gloom feeling cornered, his world crumbling around him. Sitting there with the engine still running, he briefly considered a carbon monoxide exit. Pretty clean, completely painless, easy to do—but who needed clean, painless, and easy at this juncture? Clean would not only signify guilt on Sanders's part, but it would also absolve Bissell of guilt in the mess he had started. No way was he checking out without taking Bissell with him, at least metaphorically. No, there was a better way. And if Dags Bissell was the only one who realized the method to his madness, then mission accomplished. He turned the car off.

He began to calm down as his resolve strengthened and the shadowed solitude enveloped him. The afternoon sunlight streaked through the two garage windows like a faded musical score without the notes, quite similar to his soon-to-be-extinguished life. He relaxed against the headrest, allowing a cynical sigh to escape as he recounted the promise of his youth followed by the reality of failure in his wasted life. His family was gone, Clyde was dead, and for all intents and purposes, his life was ruined—and soon it too would be gone.

There was no other way. He opened the car door, focused on his final act, and wandered into the house.

It was dark inside. He didn't bother turning on the lights as he made his way to the den, the shadows of the house fortifying his depression. He reflected on his failures, relishing the hopelessness they inspired while fortifying his resolve to move forward.

He checked his messages. Joanne had called again. He had to get her off his back before he did anything, so he returned the call.

She answered like she had been sitting next to the phone.

"Joanne, it's me, Merle. How are you feeling?"

"Can I come over, Merle? I am so lonely, and this house is so depressing. I swear I can still smell the gunpowder in the basement. I'm scared, and I haven't been able to sleep."

"Can you come by now? I'm pretty busy."

"I'll be over in fifteen minutes. Thanks. I'll make it up to you."

Merlin guessed the Xanax he'd prescribed for her after Clyde's death was having minimal effect. He needed to up the dose. He couldn't really blame her; seeing a loved one's mangled head was something he wouldn't wish on anyone. That is, until today. He needed to show her some compassion, get her temporarily wound down with some weed (ironically, Clyde's weed), and then send her home with some sleep medication and the remainder of the weed. He certainly wouldn't need it tomorrow.

He turned on some lights, rolled a joint, poured a scotch, and while he waited for Joanne, began sorting through the mail he had been ignoring for days. He was simply going through the motions when a letter caught his eye. He recognized Clyde's bold writing: a letter from the grave. Should he open it now or wait? He subtly pushed it under a magazine as the front door opened and Joanne nearly ran in. He met her in the front hall.

"Thanks for seeing me, Merle. God, I'm so sorry for the constant calls. I'm just so scared. I haven't been alone in years, and every little noise startles me. Every night I see him in the shadows. Sometimes he's healthy; sometimes he's shattered, with blood everywhere. When I sleep, I dream I've found him again and I wake up sobbing." She began pacing, lighting up a cigarette without even asking.

"Joanne, please try to relax. Come into the den and make yourself comfortable. I don't have any wine, but I do have some liquor. Would you like vodka?"

"Sure, sure, that's fine."

Shit, she was making him nervous, and his curiosity over Clyde's letter was getting the best of him. He decided to withhold it from Joanne until he'd had a chance to read it.

"Please sit."

She did, but then she immediately rose again and began pacing around the room, aggressively smoking her cigarette, looking at the bookcases while flicking ashes onto the floor, and staring at his photos and art without seeing anything. He poured her a drink, now realizing she was quite manic.

He brought her the drink, and she gulped half of it while still standing, finishing it shortly thereafter. He took the glass and refilled it. If this is what it took to calm her, he would do it.

Her breathing was slowing when he returned, and this time she sat on the couch without prompting. He sat next to her, lit up the joint, and silently passed it to her, watching as she inhaled. She began coughing, so he helped her raise the glass to her lips. She drank greedily and then took a smaller hit before returning the joint to him.

After a couple of minutes of alternating between the joint and her drink, she asked for a refill. She was calming down but getting hammered in the process. What was he going to do with her? He was getting pretty hammered himself. He didn't want her to stay but couldn't ask her to leave, and so he offered her a Valium and took one as well. They toasted Clyde and threw back the remainder of their drinks.

He began to appreciate the symmetry of his decision, and he laughed quietly as he refilled their drinks. He thought about his lunch with Bissell, how each of them was consumed with guilt over Clyde's death, and Bissell's parting words about "never wanting to see that fucking bitch again" hovered in the air. Now that bitch was here, and with any luck, soon Bissell would be too.

His plan was too good to be true. He figured he could stash Joanne upstairs, as she'd be unconscious from the booze and the drugs. He would then coerce Bissell to come by to read the letter. Then he would shoot himself with Bissell watching—and maybe, just maybe, Joanne would wake up and find Bissell standing over his second dead body in less than a week. He chuckled again, thinking, *You can't make this shit up,* and returned to the couch. He was approaching the brink of the abyss, and he embraced the feeling. He had never felt as alive as he did now, choreographing his death. What a sick life he led—enjoying, even anticipating, the promise of death. Again he laughed at the absurdity of it all.

Joanne nearly fell into him as he sat down next to her. Giggling, she asked what he was laughing about, and without waiting for an answer she began caressing his arm. His antenna went up. Was she actually hitting on him? He gently took hold of her hand, not sure what to do.

She looked at him with glazed eyes and began to weep. "I haven't been with a man for a long time—for years, I think. All Clyde and I ever did was get fucked up and crash. The intimacy left a long time ago. He couldn't fuck; he didn't want to fuck me. I didn't know how much I wanted a man until now."

She dried her eyes and gave Sanders a "fuck me now" look that he couldn't ignore in his inebriated state. He brought her closer and began caressing her shoulder, moving his hand to her hair and kneading her neck before bringing it around to caress her cheek. One of her hands dropped near his crotch; he didn't stop her as she began to fondle him. As she fumbled with his pants, he exhaled a long, slow breath and lay his head back against the couch. It had been a long time for him as well. *Why not go out with a bang, so to speak?* he thought as he helped her find him. He inhaled sharply as she took him in her mouth, and the more motivated she became, the more he began to enjoy it. He closed his eyes and smiled. What a day, and barely three o'clock.

It didn't take long for him to climax, followed by the expected self-loathing—an additional ingredient in his ultimate concoction.

Joanne looked up at him with a dreamy expression and asked, "Will you please fuck me now?"

He touched her cheek and replied, "Sure," completely unsure if he could. "Let's go upstairs."

He nearly had to carry her up to his room, but finally he managed to get her undressed and safely in bed. By then she was breathing with the rhythmic sound of sleep, and so he returned to the den and opened the letter.

No answer again—dammit! Okay, he'd leave a slightly panicky message alluding to the letter and ask Bissell to come by. He wouldn't even need to lie now. The letter would be motive enough to convince Bissell to come over.

A beep followed the message, and he began. "Dags, this is Merlin Sanders. I came across something from Clyde that I thought you should see. I know lunch was difficult, but what I have should make you feel better. It's a letter from the grave, so to speak. I was hoping you could stop by right away. It's a loose end I would like to tie up. Please." He left both numbers and his address and hung up. Now what?

What are you doing? he thought as he went upstairs to check on Joanne. *Why are you punishing her? She's your typical weakling who just proved she would do anything for drugs, and you were low enough to let her do it. You're pathetic.*

Joanne was lying as he had left her, lightly snoring in the kind of deep sleep she no doubt rarely experienced these days. She almost looked peaceful, but he could discern her emotional trauma as her fingers slightly twitched, seemingly acting to ward off another nightmare. That nightmare was closer than she could possibly imagine. Why was he doing this? Was Clyde about to participate posthumously in another suicide? Was Sanders subconsciously wanting her to suffer payback for the damage Clyde had caused him? He kissed her on the forehead and brushed her cheek. "Sweet dreams," he whispered, quietly closing the door.

The phone rang.

"Hey Merle, Dags Bissell," I announced. "What's up?"

A slightly strained voice greeted me from the other end. "Hi Dags; thanks for calling. Look, um, Clyde mailed me a letter he must have written shortly before he died. I received it today and thought you might want to see it."

"Is it a suicide note?"

"Yes, and a rather extensive one. I guess I could read it over the phone, but I really think you will want to see it. I'm only twenty minutes away."

My mind was racing. I needed to pick up Sterling and get her to the airport, but if he was on the way, maybe I could quickly stop by, read whatever he felt I needed to see, and then continue on. Sterling would certainly be interested.

"I'll try to be there within the hour," I replied as I wrote down his address.

Sanders moved into the den, withdrew the gun from the drawer, again marveling at its deadly beauty, and reread the letter.

Hey Doc,

Yeah, it's me, the dead guy. I bet this is a first for you. First for me too, and the last. I know my death is imminent, moments away, maybe. I've gotten too tired fighting to live. It's not worth it to me anymore.

You're my only remaining friend, really the only one I can still reach out to. Everyone else has deserted me. First Bissell, that nosy prick, then all of his friends and family, all gone. Pete's gone. I think Joanne is next. That leaves you, pal.

Do you remember Jamaica, when we first met? Three relatively normal families back then. Then all hell broke loose. What a blast, but the beginning of the end, at least for me. We were insatiable with the drugs, but I came to realize that the pain meds were just too strong for me. They overpowered me. I could and did handle every drug thrown my way until the Percs. That got me. That's why I'm about to do what you now already know I did.

It wasn't Dagger. It wasn't my family, although they're all pricks. It wasn't Pete. Merle, I especially want you to know that it wasn't you. It was me. However I spin this, my death can only be attributed to me and my addictions. I used to have so much fun trying to kill myself, but this time I'm deadly serious. There is no way out of this for me. It's the only way. I have no choice, but I will welcome the end. When that bullet hits my brain, my last breath will be one of relief.

Please don't harbor any guilt about my death. We were all big boys in this, and we each chose our own ride.

Joanne's going to need you after I'm gone. Try to keep an eye on her. You know how terrified of life she is. She's quite fragile, actually, but she's been my playmate in all this for a long time. I dragged her down with me and am leaving her so abruptly.

Oh, watch out for Bissell. I know he blames you for my addictions. What an idiot! If the fucker opened his eyes, he would see the truth. We are what we make ourselves. People and events influence our lives, but ultimately we succeed or fail without anybody's help.

I remember one drunken night you, Pete, and I fantasized how we would kill ourselves. I forgot what you guys said, but I said I was going out on a massive cocktail of every drug I ever liked, which was all of them. Well, I lied, didn't I?

This has been the most lucid I have been in years, but I need to wrap this up. It was a great ride, wasn't it? An unbelievable trip that now must end. Don't be pissed, and for God's sake don't be bummed. I'm only doing what needs to be done. Your bud till the end—

Clyde

Sanders read the letter again, wondering why the guilt he felt had not been shaken, had not wavered with Clyde's apology. It was still firmly entrenched between his depression and his failures in life, blurring and attaching itself to the two, the three strands weaving together to form an insurmountable obstacle to regaining the sanity he needed to live.

He had certainly honored Clyde's request to look after Joanne. Yeah, what a friend. She would probably remember nothing of the inconsequential sex act she performed. Christ, he might as well have given her Rohypnol.

He began to reexamine the gun, again moving it from one hand to the other. Beautiful balance, exquisite craftsmanship.

He placed the barrel in his mouth and inadvertently inhaled, nearly gagging. He felt the trigger. Were his feelings similar to what Clyde felt? Did Clyde put ever-so-slight pressure on the trigger, curious to see if it would fire or not, ambivalent about either result?

He exhaled as he pulled the gun from his mouth and began to hyperventilate. What a charge! Clyde must have been flying when he executed his dry run. Never had Sanders felt like this. It felt like a game of Russian roulette with himself: too much pressure, you lose; not enough, an opportunity to lose later.

What kind of scene would he create if he first shot Bissell, and maybe Joanne too, before shooting himself? Christ, he needed to get hold of himself. Sure, killing them would make it easier to kill himself, but then he would be labeled a crazy mass murderer, and his act would somehow be cheapened. No, timing was everything today, and Bissell would be his witness.

He returned to the bar for a scotch and another joint and waited.

I arrived at Beth's a little early, eager to get Sterling moving. She was already packed when Beth met me at the door. I didn't need to burden her with news of the letter, so I casually asked Sterling if she would mind leaving early, as I had an errand to run. The sisters hugged, and then they hugged again. They both had tears in their eyes as Sterling pulled away, giving her sister one last kiss. Beth turned to me.

"Dags, I haven't seen Sterling this happy in years, and I think I owe it all to you." She hugged me tight, saying, "Thank you, and please stay in touch. We're nearly neighbors."

"Thanks for everything, Beth, and we will keep in touch. I think you and Katy would really hit it off."

And that was it. I took in the surroundings once more and then grabbed Sterling's bag and headed for the car.

"Thanks again for the lift," Sterling said as we pulled out of the driveway onto Burnt Mill Road. "A very fulfilling yet complicated week is coming to a close."

As much as I wanted her to wax poetic, I didn't have the time. I needed to tell her about the letter.

"The week just became a lot more complicated," I said. "Merlin Sanders just called me about a letter he received from Clyde today. He wants me to come by."

Sterling shot me a troubled look. "Today? When did he send it? Do you know what he said?"

"I don't have the answer to any of your questions," I replied.

"What are you going to do?"

"I was hoping you might be interested in stopping by Sanders's house. It's on the way." I recognized her look, so I added some enticement. "Who knows? Who we see and what we read may provide a wealth of creative fodder for a talented writer like you. How about it? One last walk on the wild side before your return to Florida?"

The enticement apparently did little to assuage her concern.

"I don't know if I really want or need to meet this doctor or take a walk on the wild side again. The letter is a lure, though. I realize this is something you need to do, so let's go by the house and I'll wait in the car. You can fill me in on the way to the airport."

A tempered agreement was good enough for me.

Twenty minutes later, we approached his house—a typical suburban home about fifty years old that reflected the style of its era, with a beautifully laid fieldstone exterior on the first floor, white horizontal siding on the second, and dark-green ornamental shutters framing each window. Thoughtfully selected, mature shrubbery lined the oval driveway, which had an ell to the double garage doors on the side of the house. I drove just past the front door, killed the engine, and glanced at Sterling. She took my hand.

"Good luck—and hurry. Remember, I have a plane to catch."

"I'll be back" was all I could say, using my bad Arnold imitation to ease her concern. As I exited the car, another, vaguely familiar car caught my eye, but the thought didn't crack my preoccupied mind.

Sanders was finishing his drink when he heard the doorbell. He checked the gun one last time and placed it back in the den drawer with the letter from Clyde. He inhaled through his nose and began a slow exhale for relaxation and focus before slowly walking to the front door. He took another slow breath before opening it.

When Sanders opened the door, I knew something was wrong. He looked like shit. His eyes were glazed and bloodshot, he smelled of alcohol, and the pungent aroma of weed spilled out from the house. I like weed. At another time and with another person, I might have smelled it and looked forward to the coming moments. Not now, though. This visit was a reluctant response to a request from a man I'd hoped never to see again.

He seemed to sense my unease. "Please come in, Dags."

"Are you okay?" I asked.

"As you can imagine, I've had a tough day. Please, come in."

I shrugged and followed him to the rear of the house and into what was certainly his den. The room was naturally dark, dominated by an antique oak rolltop desk. On top of the desk was an ashtray in which a roach was still smoldering. A rocks glass sat on a recessed bar nearby. He offered me a seat on a small leather couch.

"Do you smoke, Dags?"

"Not today, thanks. I'm driving to the airport."

"So a drink is out of the question?"

I nodded.

He opened a drawer and withdrew the letter, partially closing the drawer before turning toward me. He seemed to be agitated as he handed it to me.

"I received this today. I would like you to read it."

I took the letter and began to read. "Hey Doc. Yeah, it's me, the dead guy." I looked at Sanders; he looked troubled. I felt worse. "I bet this is a first for you. First for me too, and the last." I was reliving my old friend's suicide. Why? Why read what I already knew? I tried to force myself to look away, but failed. "I know my death is imminent, moments away, maybe." Had Clyde already called me at this point? Was I not his last contact? I began to read blindly, absorbing nothing. He wasn't the first to call me a nosy prick, and he certainly wouldn't be the last.

I stopped when I read that he no longer blamed me, at least for that moment: "It wasn't Dags."

I met Sanders's gaze as he fired a shot over my left shoulder, hitting a hardback book that had been sitting on the bookshelf behind me. The second shot blew out the window behind my right shoulder. The noise was deafening.

Sterling was reminiscing about her week when she thought she heard a shot. The second one got her attention with the shattering of glass; she instinctively opened the car door and ran toward the front door. The third shot seemed to come from deep within the house. She tried the door. It was open. She quietly turned the knob and entered as the fourth shot echoed through the house.

She took a deep breath as she surveyed her surroundings. She was facing the stairs as a half-naked woman appeared, standing unsteadily on the second-floor landing. Sterling recognized her but couldn't place her. She made eye contact with the woman and raised a finger to her own lips. The woman looked scared and lost, but she obeyed Sterling's signal. As the fifth shot was fired, Sterling took the fourteen steps two at a time to reach her.

She could hear voices from below, a good sign that Dags was still alive. She assumed that the other voice was Sanders's. It was manic in tone, sometimes rising to a scream before falling again to a muted growl.

The woman next to her seemed to be in shock—paralyzed with fear and barely breathing, with the unfocused expression of incomprehension. She was clutching Sterling's wrist, her nails digging into the skin, when suddenly Sterling recognized her as the woman from the church, Joanne Colson.

Sterling grabbed her chin, trying to bring her back to reality, and whispered, "Who is downstairs? How many people, and where are they?"

Joanne could only mumble that she didn't know.

"Don't move," Sterling said. Then she crept back down to the first-floor landing and followed the voices around the corner. She heard Dags plead, "Don't do it!" and then his scream as a thunderous roar overwhelmed her.

The first shot didn't register with me—I had never been shot at, so my brain was slow to digest the information—but the second one caused me to drop the letter and search Sanders's face for a reason. He smiled at me.

"How is your reading going? Please don't let me interrupt you." He casually fired another shot into the couch. "What? You can't concentrate on what your late old friend is trying to say? Let me quickly paraphrase his letter for you." His voice began to rise as he moved around the confined space. "What he doesn't say is how many lives you have ruined with your holier-than-thou attitude. What he doesn't say is, 'Who put you in charge of how we treat ourselves?'" He stopped moving and slowly pointed the gun at me. "Today one of us dies and one of us lives. Who will the lucky one be? Will the one who lives be able to continue unscarred, or will he be unlucky after all?" His laugh was insane.

Sanders began handling the gun the way a conductor might handle a baton, languidly waving at the strings to participate, then turning and motioning to the horns for some light accompaniment, and finally alternating between pointing the gun at me and then back at himself. He was so disjointed that I could only sit and stare as he rambled on.

"Will the guy who dies be the one who attains salvation? Hah! Interesting theory, don't you think, Mr. Dags Bissell?" His voice was rising again. "By killing you, will I save you? Will the guy who lives be forever tortured? Look at yourself! Can you handle two blown-out brains in one week? Here we go," he said, bringing the gun to his head. He was staring right through me.

I managed a weak "Please don't do this" as he cocked the gun and put it next to his temple. He angled it back and fired, missing his head by an inch, and burst into shrill giggles.

"You can't take seeing another man shoot himself in the head, now can you? Answer me! Can you?"

I shook my head.

He resumed the gun twirling. "I didn't think so. Clyde had hallucinations of a dragon that ultimately tortured him to death.

Well, that dragon now haunts me." He moved toward the leather easy chair facing me. "Does it haunt you yet, or are you too above the fray to allow that? Don't you think there's a little of the dragon in each of us? There is some in me, and I see it in you too, Bissell. Come on, don't you see it? Can't you smell its acrid breath? Breathe in its fire? It's here, in this room with us. Can't you feel it?" He closed his eyes and inhaled deeply.

I simply stared.

He sat down in the chair and seemed to relax his grip on the gun. Was this my chance to save him and maybe garner salvation for myself as well? I held his gaze as I rose and said, "Merlin, don't do this to yourself. Don't do it."

He tilted his head back to meet my gaze, showing a serene face with dreamy eyes and a contented smile.

"Don't do it," I repeated, holding out my hand for the gun.

18

As the gun traveled to his chin, our eyes met. His begged for relief; mine pleaded for him to stop. Everything slowed to a cinematic crawl—my scream released too late, my reflexes far too slow to prevent the inevitable. As I reached for the gun, it exploded in front of me, the bullet spewing bone, blood, and brain matter onto my face, stinging my eyes, as it traveled through his. His dying body lurched to the floor. He was dead before I reached him, but I grabbed him anyway and hugged him as a muted scream escaped my throat. I didn't want him to leave this earth alone, as Clyde had done. If he somehow knew, even as his body was shutting down, that he was not alone, that I was there holding him as he transferred from this life to the next, then maybe, just maybe, the terror would be lessened, both for him and for me.

Someone was tugging me; the screams were not just mine. I released my grip to find Sterling kneeling next to me, pulling me away, crying as she held me, trying to force me to turn away. I couldn't. I needed to see this through. Until Sanders became completely still, I was going to share his journey. I closed my eyes and held his hand as the final twitching subsided. He was gone. I released his hand and gently laid him back on the floor.

"Are you hit? Are you hurt?" Sterling screamed in a voice I could barely hear.

I looked down and discovered blood and gray matter spattered over much of my chest. I licked my lips and tasted blood.

Mine?

His?

Did it matter?

Sterling pulled me close, shielding my eyes from a scene I hadn't escaped, and tore my shirt at the collar to check for damage. I felt no emotion as shock began to set in. My breathing slowed as I turned back to look. We were both dead. He had succeeded. One bullet had killed us both.

A moan from the hall reached the den. I glanced through the doorway to see Joanne huddled on the floor, a shawl wrapped tightly around her shoulders, failing to protect her. She couldn't see Sanders, but his mess was inescapable, and as reality set in, she too began to withdraw into shock. Joanne and I, bitter enemies, wedded to two suicides in a week. Another forever moment dragging me closer to my unforgettable abyss.

I was powerless—couldn't move, couldn't run to her and hold her as I had Sanders. She didn't mean anything to me now, but I touched Sterling and nodded Joanne's way. Sterling understood and pushed herself up to go to her. Sterling had smears of blood on her face, shoulders, and hands from hugging me, but the enormity of the moment precluded any cleanup. There was blood and debris everywhere.

My ears were ringing as I crawled to the phone to call the police. Unsure if I could hear a voice, I dialed 911. I wondered what the police department would think about me, the chronic suicide caller. Would I be a guy in the wrong place at the wrong time again? A killer who'd created a suicide scene? Or simply a man with weird friends who liked to die in front of him? Whatever. I made the call.

The blood-misted letter caught my eye as the dispatcher identified herself and asked me the nature of my problem. Should I just come out and say that I was a witness to another suicide, that I knew dysfunctional people, that I was the dark clown in that parade? Or should I just spit out the facts?"

Simple won.

"A man has just shot himself. He's dead." I left the address and hung up.

I didn't want to talk to her anymore. She could trace the call and send someone if she wanted to. I really didn't care whether she sent someone or not. A guy was dead, and having someone verify that fact, take statements, and take him away meant nothing to me. A man I had grown to hate over many years, a man I had wanted to kill just a few days before, lay blood-spattered on the floor. Suddenly I cared. I hadn't wanted to, hadn't planned to, but when a life bleeds away in your arms, you have no choice but to care.

I turned to Sterling. "I've got to call Katy."

Sterling nodded.

I made the call.

She answered on the second ring.

Not knowing what to say or how to say it, I simply let the words cascade out in a torrent of unbridled emotion. I told her how much I loved her, how much I had always loved her, and how lucky I had always felt being with her.

"Dags, honey, what's wrong?" Katy asked sensing something catastrophic. "You sound so far away."

"I'm at Sanders's house. Sanders just shot himself." Again, I opted for simple. I would tell her about Sterling and Joanne later. How could I muster the courage to give her the details of the shooting? How could I replay that scene for anyone? My statement to the cops would require it, but after that, I didn't know if I had the emotional strength to relive it again. I guessed that when she saw me she would understand.

"Where does he live? I'll be right over," Katy said with untapped resolve in her voice.

"He lives too far away. Honey, look, the cops are here, and things will be wrapping up soon. I'll be home before you know it." I told another protective lie about the cops before ending with a heartfelt "I love you, dear." So simple, so true.

While Sterling was caring for Joanne, I began to reread the letter. "It wasn't Dags." I didn't want to read any further, and I didn't mind his calling me a prick. The fact was, I had been a prick to Clyde even while we were friends, and certainly these last several months. But "It wasn't Dags" was what I'd wanted to hear him say. I continued reading until Clyde took ownership of his actions: "My death can only be attributed to me and my addictions." Who was this guy, and why did he make that call to me when he had just written a letter to Sanders taking full responsibility? Was he capable of lucidity one moment and uncontrolled rage the next, or was he simply spinning two scenarios for his own enigmatic reasons?

I looked over at Sanders and felt an odd sense of envy. Here was a man who'd been about to kill himself, and this letter granted him salvation from guilt for eternity if he chose it. Yet Sanders chose to eschew Clyde's pardon and proceed with his twisted conclusion.

Clyde, my old friend, had unknowingly tried to save Sanders's life and shortly thereafter had tried to take mine, at least figuratively. At the end of the letter, he said he was only taking care of business—such a detached way to explain self-murder.

The final words of Clyde's letter were beginning to blur from the pink mixture of my tears and Sanders's blood. I suddenly needed to move. The pool of blood from Sanders was advancing and beginning to touch my shoes. I rose and found the powder room around the corner, but I was interrupted by the sirens. Not wanting to be the next victim, I went to the front door and opened it. I didn't know where Sterling and Joanne were.

Two cops with guns drawn opened their car doors and, using them as shields, instructed me to lie down on the ground. I complied and waited patiently as they cuffed me and pulled me to my feet. Next Sterling and Joanne appeared at the door, Sterling giving Joanne a nurturing hug. Their appearance didn't alter the cops' protocol, except instead of having to lie down, the women were asked to face the wall with their hands above them. They too complied as another cruiser drove up. By now the scene had gotten the attention of the neighborhood as two SWAT officers approached Sterling and asked about the disturbance. She remained calm and told them that the owner of the house had committed suicide and could be found in the den, located behind the stairs to the left. One of the first officers escorted the women to a cruiser, and once they were safely seated in the back, he signaled for the SWAT team to clear the house. Moments later they reappeared, and an ambulance was summoned to the front door. I was led to another cruiser, where I was checked for wounds as I made a detailed statement before asking if I could clean up in the kitchen. An officer escorted me to the kitchen sink and allowed me to wash my hands and face.

As I let the water warm, I reflected on the Lady Macbeth analogy I'd contemplated in the shower so very long ago. Was it yesterday, the day before, or a lifetime ago? As I washed my face, the water turned dark pink, and as it cascaded down my face into the sink, some inadvertently touched my mouth. I did not recoil as Sanders's blood entered the capillaries of my taste buds. I simply began to sob.

The logistics of our situation demanded cooler heads. What should we do with Joanne? She was still in shock, and Sterling hadn't been able to get her to say anything. I quietly approached an EMT and alerted him to my suspicions of her extreme drug use and possible suicidal tendencies. He ordered another ambulance to the scene, and she was taken to a local hospital. I gave him her address so a tow truck could deliver her car to her house.

Sterling had already missed her flight, so I offered to drive her back home. It was a slow, quiet ride. We didn't speak. I had dragged her into my problems for a chance to glean some literary inspiration, but being a witness to a shooting was not the creative reward she had been expecting. I think whatever fascination I'd held in her eyes disintegrated when she heard Sanders fire his final shot.

When we reached Beth's house, all I could say was "I'm sorry." All I got in return was "Yeah." She brought her hand to my face, touching my cheek lightly and then kissing it before turning toward the house and slowly walking away. She didn't look back. I waited until she had disappeared inside before beginning the drive home. I tried to assemble the images of the day into a collage of events that had drawn each of us to Sanders's house that afternoon. The resulting, schizophrenic picture bled chaos.

Sterling and Joanne were the innocents in this climactic scene. This was a dance only Sanders and I should have choreographed. Why was Joanne there at all, and why was she upstairs? Certainly they weren't having an affair, were they, so soon after Clyde's death? Why would he kill himself with her upstairs unless she had somehow surprised him? I would never know.

Sterling had been my responsibility. I had reacted so flippantly to Sanders's request that I had overlooked safety issues that had nearly gotten both Sterling and me killed. Had Sanders accidently hit me with a shot, he most likely would have finished the job, and with Sterling at the door, he undoubtedly would have panicked and killed her too. Madeleine would have been orphaned simply because I was selfish in my desire for her mother.

Katy met me at the door and involuntarily recoiled when she saw me. I followed her eyes to my chest. I was still covered in dried blood, the sins of my soul displayed on my body like a scarlet letter. When our eyes met, she rushed to me and hugged me tight.

"Are you hurt?" she asked as she led me inside.

"Not physically," I replied. Needing to lighten the situation, I added, "You oughta see what the other guy looks like."

"Stop talking like that. I'm going to get you cleaned up, right now."

She led me to the laundry room and stripped off my clothes until I was naked. Then she led me upstairs to our bathroom and began drawing a tub. It looked so inviting, and when I entered, the different layers of the day began melting away. Katy played wife, nurse, therapist, and lover as she cleaned my body and began to nurture my soul back to health.

"What happened today?" she finally asked when she knew I was ready to talk.

"After our lunch, as you know, Sanders called about a letter. I stashed it in my pants pocket, so please save it. In the letter, Clyde absolved everyone, including me, of any guilt, laying it at his own feet. That was the good part." I stopped talking and groaned as Katy began massaging my neck and shoulders with a soapy loofah. "The weird thing is that I don't think the letter was the lure to get me over there. I think Sanders had another sinister plan and the letter was coincidental good luck that happened to fall into his lap. He wanted to scare the living shit out of me before shooting himself in front of me—probably some sort of bizarre payback for my responsibility in Clyde's death." I looked up to meet Katy's eyes. "This is a man I could have killed for what he did to Clyde, and he ends up trying to kill me by killing himself. What is it with these guys? Does Percocet addiction lead to discovering creative ways to kill yourself? He shot at me three, four, five times, I don't remember, before turning the gun on himself. He was so enraged that I felt each shot might hit me, but that was never his intent. His intent was to blow his brains out with me watching, and he succeeded spectacularly."

Each time I considered sparing Katy the uncomfortable details, I ended up spilling my guts to her anyway. With that in mind, I continued. "Katy, Sterling was there. I could have gotten her killed. I almost got my daughter's mother killed. For what? To satisfy some personal vendetta of mine?" The words spilled out too quickly to allow any interruptions. "I tasted his blood. Katy, I fucking tasted Sanders's blood. It was all over my face!" I grabbed the loofah and began scrubbing my face as I burst into tears.

Katy stopped her massage and gently drew me close, caressing my neck as her tacit response. Calming down, I drew a slow breath.

"The weird thing is that I wasn't repulsed. When his blood got in my mouth, it was like we were experiencing a final connection, like he was allowing me in to experience the core of his existence and the finality of his death." Katy moaned and drew me closer.

Revitalizing and wanting to move forward, I related the dark comedy of my statement to the police:

> *Why did he shoot at you, Mr. Bissell?*
> *To scare the shit out of me, I imagine.*
> *Why was he angry with you?*
> *Because he believed I killed his friend.*

Did you kill somebody that we don't know about, Mr. Bissell?
No. We had a mutual friend who committed suicide last week. He felt I might have had something to do with it.
Who was the suicide victim?
Clyde Colson. I discovered the body.
Let me get this straight. You've witnessed two suicides in a week?
I guess I'm just lucky. Maybe I should play the lottery.

"You should have seen his face when I gave him a thumbnail sketch of Clyde's relationship to me and Sanders. He was so confused that he gave me the typical line cops use when they don't want to be seen being confused: 'Okay, that will be all for now, Mr. Bissell, but I advise you not to leave town until we have this wrapped up.' I poked him once more by saying, 'Officer, it is wrapped up. Sanders is dead by suicide, and if I fucking want to leave town, I will. Now, if you don't have any more inane questions, I need to get home to my wife.'" I looked up at Katy and smiled. "And here I am. Lucky you!" Then I splashed water in her face.

Later that night we made love. It wasn't overly passionate, but more gentle and caring, with short kisses and long caresses as we enveloped each other while isolating the world outside. We were one as we explored familiar territory, excited nonetheless by our intimate discoveries. The night was our affirmation of our marriage commitment to each other.

When we were done, I tried to sleep. I dozed off only to have Merlin's corpse return as an apparition, headless save for a smile where the mouth should have been. The smile transformed into a laugh, and the body morphed into a skeleton and began to dance herky-jerky style, awkwardly and out of sync. The skeleton suddenly broke off the dance in mid-jig, stared at me through dark, sightless eyes, and began to spew fire through its bony mouth. A gun materialized in its right hand, and as I let out a fruitless scream, it brought the gun up and leveled it at me, laughing, before turning it upon itself and pulling the trigger. The explosion shattered its skull, and blood splashed toward me. I was tasting it again, I was smelling it, and I was choking on it as I awoke to the sounds of my panicked breathing. I licked my lips. The blood was gone. I turned to hug Katy. She was sound asleep, so I gently drew her close as I willed the skeleton away. Sanders disappeared, and only then did I sleep.

The phone rang. I stirred as it rang again. I reached over and fumbled with it in the dark, wondering who could be calling so late. I mumbled hello, and the ghostlike voice of Clyde responded with "Hey Dagger. It's me. Why did you let me kill myself? I needed you, and you let me down."

"Clyde," I mumbled, "I didn't know you were sick."

He was crying for help.

I told him to wait, to let me come over so we could talk. I told him I loved him. I told him to hang on.

He said it was too late; he was already dead.

Again I said, "Wait," and then I hung up the phone and tried to get out of bed. I knew I needed to get over to his house to save him, but my legs wouldn't move, and my voice made no sound.

I crawled to the car, but I couldn't start it. Where were the keys? There they were, in my hand, but they didn't fit the ignition. What should I do?

I began to run, an awkward run like the skeleton's lurching dance, tripping over my feet and crashing into trees and walls that suddenly materialized before me.

I was in quicksand, sinking. I lay down and began to swim.

When I looked up, the dragon was charging right at me, fire spewing from its nostrils and mouth. I ducked beneath the quicksand, and when I could no longer hold my breath, I tentatively exhaled and then inhaled the moist sand. I didn't choke. I was breathing under the sand. I stayed submerged as I began to swim toward Clyde's house. *Hurry—not much time. Gotta save my friend.*

Somehow I arrived, crashing through his front door and nearly falling down the steps to his basement. He was there, sitting on the blankets, caressing Bear and smoking a cigarette, a drink nearby. The gun lay by his side. I had gotten there in time!

He looked at me and asked why I was there.

I sat beside him and began to hug him as I cried. That's what friends do, I said; they help their friends.

He replied that he hadn't thought I would come, that I should hate him for what he had said.

I told him that I'd never stopped loving him and would always be there for him.

As he misted away, I pleaded with him not to go, but he wasn't listening.

My crying woke Katy, who hugged me. "Dags, it's okay. Everything's okay. I'm here."

My crying intensified as I realized that I had not gotten there in time, that Clyde was so assuredly and so obviously dead and gone forever.

Katy strengthened her hold on me, whispering that she would never let go. She continued to hold me until I cried myself to sleep.

My father appeared as he had in the past, to console me and offer protection—not through his words, which were never necessary, but by his demeanor. I was a young boy again, needing a hug from my dad. He embraced me the way a father would embrace a son he had not seen in years. We both knew he was dead, and I knew I was in another dream when we both began to cry; my father never cried in front of me when he was alive. I didn't want to let go, but he gently pushed me away, his eyes saying that everything would be fine, that he had always been proud of me, that he was especially proud of me now.

Again I awoke, soaked in sweat and exhausted from the barrage of dreams. Katy was still holding me, as she had promised she would. I prayed she would never let go. I lay there afraid to sleep, terrified by the promise of another phantom visitor. I was still awake when the dark of night gave way to gray. Only then did I finally sleep.

19

A warm morning breeze off the gulf rustled the curtains as it gently blew into Sterling's office and seemed to alight at her desk like an apparition, stirring her from her reverie. She sighed and rose to fetch herself a Diet Coke.

She had been in a trance since her return from Delaware two weeks ago. Her writer's block was slowly dissipating as she struggled to regain normalcy, albeit a new normalcy. Her life was forever changed, but she recognized that change was the essence of life. She gently wiped a tear from her eye as she reflected on those changes, which enveloped the full spectrum of her journey—from finding a lost love to watching him nearly die to witnessing the death of the man who had nearly killed him. And yet that tear had created a small, unconscious smile.

Distance. She needed the distance of time to understand what a unique adventure she had experienced. She needed the distance of emotion to clarify her current feelings about her recent journey. And she needed patience until that distance arrived and she could begin her life anew.

Time and distance were the elixir she needed to deal with this new chapter. Every day gained her more of the distance she sought, and every day brought clarity a little closer. Every day drew the sanity she'd believed she had lost back into her soul. She knew that because that inward smile today had been her first.

After the shooting, Sterling had exited Dags's car with barely a "see ya," much as he had exited her life so many years ago. Bethany wasn't home, so she had been able to wash her clothes enough to throw them out without anyone noticing the bloodstains. Then she took a long, cleansing shower punctuated by uncontrolled sobbing as she relived those last moments at Sanders's house.

She had heard their voices, primarily Sanders's, as she crept closer to the partially opened door. As the room came into view, she heard a scream and, at the same moment, a shot that was more muffled than the others had been. The scream continued as she pushed the door open to see Dags grab Sanders, who was obviously dead. Dags was holding Sanders, screaming, "No, no, no !" and then she began to scream when she saw that Dags was covered in blood. She wondered if he had been shot too, and was alarmed that he may have done the shooting.

The scene was horrific, the stench of gunpowder and blood pervading the room, a nightmare come to life—one man covered in blood, the other without a face. She tried to pull Dags away, but he refused and continued to hold Sanders. He gestured toward the hall; she recognized Joanne and went to her, wanting to help, needing to escape. She gently took hold of Joanne and led her to the kitchen, where they sat on the floor together, huddling close while Joanne whimpered like a small, scared animal. They sat there, not saying anything, until they heard the sirens.

Sterling slowly made her way out to the porch and sat down in a cushioned, wicker rocking chair facing the courtyard and, beyond that, the gulf. The aromas carried by the breeze portended a crisp, low-humidity day. Her cardinals were still chasing each other from palm to palm, and the mockingbirds were doing what they do best, mimicking the cardinals. Above, an osprey flew past holding a terrified fish, both on their way to breakfast. She marveled at her life and allowed herself another smile, this one more overt.

She grabbed her phone and called Madeleine, hoping to catch her before work. She was in luck; a slightly out-of-breath girl answered.

"Hi Mom. What's up? I'm running around getting ready to go to the beach."

"No work today?"

"Nope, I'm taking the day off. They let me do that occasionally when things are slow. How are you?"

"Honey, I am doing so well," Sterling said. "It's a gorgeous morning, the birds are singing, the lizards are darting around flapping their fans, and I seem to be cultivating a smile." With that she let out a laugh.

"Boy, Mom, you do sound happy. Did you meet someone?"

"Ha-ha, dear; I think meeting someone right now is pretty low on my to-do list. The last guy almost got himself killed." She caught herself laughing before taking a moment to reflect on her time with Dags. She continued in a more serious tone. "But that was yesterday, honey, and today is a new day."

Sterling had been concerned about how much she should tell Madeleine about her last couple of days in Delaware. Madeleine was young, still quite innocent, and celebrating the discovery of her father. The details of Sanders's death were something Sterling had seriously considered withholding from Madeleine, until she realized that she had done the same thing with Madeleine about the identity of her father. With that in mind, she had insisted that Madeleine come down for another sunset and sleepover. Over a bottle of Simi chardonnay, Sterling had gently broached the subject of Sanders's suicide, slowly stirring in answers as questions were asked. She held back nothing, and as the sunset deepened into night, Madeleine learned everything. Her father had inadvertently almost gotten her mother killed.

Sterling, who was adamant about moving forward from Clyde's funeral, had chosen not to contact Dags. She believed that he had neither the time nor the inclination to stay in touch with her, and she was loath to approach him. He was an emotionally dangerous guy whom she needed to avoid. She shuddered as she remembered what he had done to her, both twenty-five years ago and two weeks ago. He no longer held the title of knight in shining armor. On the other hand, he was Madeleine's father.

"Have you heard from your father?"

"Not yet, Mom. Do you think I will? After all he has been through, I don't think he ever wants to see me again."

Sterling began to twirl her hair as she moved about the courtyard trying to justify his silence to her daughter.

"Of course he does, Madeleine. At some point he will reach out to you. I know he will, but only he knows when. He has experienced a very rough stretch full of confusion and tragedy. I think that once he gets his house in order, so to speak, and begins to feel healed from what has happened, you will hear from him." Sterling left unsaid her conviction that there was no way Dags was going to run away again, even if she had to go back to Delaware and drag his ass back to Florida to see Madeleine.

"I hope so. I kinda liked him, and he was very funny. I enjoyed being around him. But he seems to be a lightning rod for trouble, from what little I've seen and heard. God, what are the chances of finding two people dead in a week?"

Sterling gently replied, "However high those odds are, they shrink according to the instability of the people you associate with. For a period there, he associated with the wrong people, and he paid a serious price. He is very lucky to be alive." Sterling thought for a moment before continuing. "You know, Madeleine, you could always call him. I've got his number. I'm sure he would love to hear from you."

"Yeah, maybe in a while. I don't know. What are you doing today?"

"Honey, I'm going to try to finish my book. The last couple of days have been fertile in the creativity department, and today may be the day."

"Have you thought of a title yet?"

Sterling paused and gazed beyond the courtyard. "I think I may call it *The Room Beckoned*."

They talked for another ten minutes, planning Easter in Boca Grande, and promised to talk again the next day. When Sterling hung up, she decided to work outside and let nature inspire her. She opened her laptop and began to write.

They stretched out on the beach, eager to enjoy this final, magical moment. Today would be different than their passionate culinary fantasy from before. Today would mark the end.

The sand began to cool as the sun made its way down to the horizon, but the warmth of their bodies so close kept the spell alive. She lightly ran her fingers along his taut upper body and began circling his chest with her forefinger before opening her hand and creating an invisible pattern around his navel. She saw a stirring within his bathing suit and moved her hand to his face. He grabbed her finger and brought it into his mouth. She gently withdrew it and began to run it along his unshaven jaw.

"Have you ever seen the green flash from the sunset?" she asked, nudging closer.

"Once," he replied, "in Barbados, many years ago. But I must have been drunk on the local rum because I haven't seen it since." He shifted toward her. "But if the legend keeps people like us together for a few more moments, then who's to argue?" He turned to kiss her cheekbone. "Maybe we'll see it tonight."

They unconsciously moved closer together, knowing this fantasy was drawing to a close. Tomorrow they would return to their lives of comfort and safety, but for now, they lingered in this moment, a moment that would stretch throughout the night, a moment they both hoped would last throughout eternity.

"Why does this happen to people?" she asked with more than a hint of frustration in her voice. "We craft and lead lives that we think work for us, and then in our final chapters, we find a love we never imagined existed. It is so unfair that the roots of our lives are too deep to cut."

They both realized, though, that life was simply life, and in all their years, they had learned to expect the unexpected while continuing to move forward.

They began to kiss, softly at first, lips barely touching, exploring and enjoying the sensory arousal of such tenderness. Then their tongues met and they were transformed within each other's souls, lost in the oneness of such a simple yet intimate act. Their bodies became one as the transformation developed, but then as quickly as it had begun, it was over. She giggled, pissing him off at first for ruining their moment. But then she nuzzled closer, nibbled on his ear, and whispered, "The room beckons."

He laughed as only she could make him do, and so began their final walk together toward their destiny.

The End

Sterling smiled as she always did when she finished one of her books, experiencing a warm glow of happiness rather than a sense of accomplishment. She mused about her real-life experience two weeks earlier and the harsh reality of her last moments with Dags Bissell. No, she didn't get the man of her dreams, at least not yet, but the father of her child had entered her life, and that in itself was a fairy-tale ending.

Surveying her surroundings, she marveled at the life she had created for herself in Boca Grande. She realized that life did not always have storybook endings, but she also knew that sometimes it did. She closed her laptop and began imagining her next romantic novel, preliminarily titled *The Brandywine River Romance*. It had already been written in her head.

20

I pulled into the gravel driveway of my aunt's house and cut the engine. I'd been under informal house arrest since the debacle at Sanders's house two months earlier, and Katy had allowed me a quick foray outside our walls only if I promised not to interact with anyone. With that in mind, I had chosen a solitary walk in the country. I believe Katy was affording me the priceless opportunity to explore my psyche, something that seemed so important to everyone but me. But if it got me out of the house, then I was certainly game for a wild goose chase.

I followed the path Sterling and I had previously explored, letting my feet lead me back to the springhouse where we had playacted my knight taking her maiden in an earlier age and a more innocent time, before I had involved her in Sanders's suicide.

Sitting on the same stone bench, this time alone and with no resemblance to that knight in shining armor, I began the search for my elusive psyche.

What a journey it had been since Clyde called to say good-bye: two men dead and countless people scarred. Was it a waste of life or simply life itself?

An unexpected chill intruded on my thoughts, and so I rose from the bench and walked back out into the clearing to let the sun rejuvenate me. The promise of an afternoon thunderstorm lingered on the horizon, but for the moment, serenity ruled.

I know I'll never get over this, and I'm not sure I even want to. Katy and I have hardly been apart since I showed up covered in somebody else's essence of life. The last couple of times that she sent me out into the world alone proved disastrous, so I'm thinking the remainder of my life will be spent under full adult supervision, with the occasional outside pass granted for good behavior. So be it.

So I've spent my days not reliving Clyde's suicide, but celebrating the fragility of life.

Hands in my pockets, eyes on the ground, I walked toward the tree where Sterling and I shared a tender kiss. I removed a hand from a pocket and gently stroked the cold bark on a lower branch, hoping to infuse the present with that moment. As I leaned against the tree, my eyes were drawn to a red-shouldered hawk that soared above me, free to glide on the fickle currents of the wind. My thoughts returned to my father and the active role he assumed to guide me to psychological safety. If I've learned anything from my dreams, it's how thin the line is between life and death, and the allure that both seem to offer.

My dear, twisted friend, Clyde, could not be saved. His makeup, his family history, his life choices, his … destiny created a distinct road that only he could travel, and it culminated in his inviting death into his life. Simply said, he was who he was, he did what he did, and he's dead. It's a chapter in my life that didn't end well, but it's only a chapter.

Sanders's suicide was different. Where Clyde had sought an escape from hell, Sanders's act seemed like a bizarre revenge pact with a devil who offered absolution for his sins. Both men had achieved the same goal while balancing on different tightropes. Clyde chose to die a solitary death, cocooned in a closet with his best friend by his side, quietly thinking thoughts we can only conjecture, never knowing when that moment would arrive—the moment when he would attain the courage to put that gun in his mouth and pull the trigger.

Sanders choreographed his final moments into a tightly woven performance, replete with a captive and interactive audience.

Both men were insane. Of that there can be no doubt.

Two phone calls—each made with a certain degree of compassion combined with a healthy dose of frustration and anger—changed the lives of so many, but from those calls sprang a discovered life and another reconnection. From death springs life, life in the form of a daughter, her life born from the womb of her mother as winter morphs into spring and moves into summer.

Two phone calls. If I'd never made the first, then the second ... well, if Clyde had chosen death by suicide, he would have left me out of it. Yet those calls initiated a series of priceless, life-changing events that if altered would somehow diminish the importance, the necessity, and the uniqueness of that rich palette we call life.

If not for those phone calls, I would still be ignorant about my daughter; I would have lived out my days never knowing about Madeleine or really even caring about Sterling. Now I'm forced to confront my juvenile actions and explore my feelings for Sterling as I strive to become a better man.

Through my dreams, my father's spirit guided me—nudging me here, protecting me there, always close, always intimate, always alive. Without the consequences of Clyde's phone call, he may never have visited me in the role of a father mentoring a young, inexperienced son. By showing me what I had missed being a father, he gave me the courage to confront my past and accept my new daughter.

The night when we cried together, I believe he was saying that he wished he were with me in life—that death was okay, but until his family was on the other side with him, he would rather be alive. He implored me to embrace life for what it is, an incredible gift that is not everlasting. Savor it, he seemed to say, for someday it will end. One day we will all confront that final breath. How will we face it? Will we even know what is happening? My father taught me to see things through his eyes, not mine. Mine were too clouded, too involved, too human.

For that reason I will never understand how Clyde and Merlin could have ended their lives as they did, in spectacular violence, and yet subliminally I will always know why they did it. Somehow the mysterious allure of suicide captivated them both, intoxicating them into believing the act might bring them redemption. All it brought them was relief. To oversimplify, they were two fucked-up guys who performed an incredibly courageous feat by blowing themselves from here to eternity. And the price they paid was enormous.

I have often imagined what might have happened had I gotten to Clyde in time, had my dream been real. Could I have helped him had I descended those basement steps sooner, or would he have pulled a Merlin and enjoyed having me as a witness to his death?

I occasionally imagine Clyde healthy, both physically and spiritually, away from his worldly vices and surrounded by loving friends and family, somehow living life the way it should be lived. Yes, I have a vivid imagination as I seek to remember him in a more innocent world.

Realistically, I doubt we could have reconciled our years-long differences and returned to the friendship of our youth. We shared an irreparably damaged relationship that would have slowly dissolved completely had he lived and I done nothing. Any possibility of reconciliation was forever lost when he said good-bye to Bear and pulled the trigger. Yet his blood-misted letter remains in my drawer, occasionally inviting me in for a visit.

A couple of thick drops of rain interrupted my thoughts as I began the slow walk back through the woods. Not quite ready to leave, I looked up at the sky searching for that hawk, and relished the increasing moisture as the rain intensified and the cleansing began anew.

I have a wife.

I have a daughter.

And I will always have my father.

I have no plans to contact Sterling.

Of course, I had no plans to participate in two suicides, either.

But sometimes you just gotta laugh, marvel at the fucking turns that life deals out, and then grab another beer, always remembering that man plans, God laughs, and between them the dragon lurks.

The End

ACKNOWLEDGMENTS

The Dragon's Fire began as a two-page story sent to a friend. That friend, Wendy Leslie, urged me to write more, gave me the courage to create, and lent a helping hand with some of the book's passages. Wendy, my limited vocabulary lacks the appropriate words to properly thank you.

When the book stalled, my old friend Don Degraff came to the rescue and offered to edit it. His ideas and positive review gave me the impetus to move forward. He was instrumental in guiding me to Lulu publishing. Thank you, Don, both for your help and for your invaluable friendship.

Thank you to Lulu publishing and their editor Allison in bringing *The Dragon's Fire* to fruition.

Finally and especially to my wife, Shelley, thank you for making me so happy and being saintlike with your patience.